"I'll bet he isn't like Gus," she whispered. "Matthew Sterling looks kind and good. According to Seth, he's as solid and true as his name."

She closed her eyes and imagined the stranger riding up to rescue her from the unspeakable future Gus and Tice planned. The next instant Sarah shook her head. "Appearances are just that—appearances. Seth might be mistaken about his friend. Even though Matthew means *gift of the Lord,* he might be no better than Gus and Tice."

Sarah sighed. If all men were like those two, she would *never* marry. Better to live alone than live married to someone she didn't love—or worse, who would never really love her the way God meant a husband to love his wife.

COLLEEN L. REECE was born and raised in a small western Washington logging town. She learned to read by kerosene lamplight and dreamed of someday writing a book. God has multiplied Colleen's "someday" book into more than 140 titles that have sold six million copies. Colleen was twice voted Heartsong Presents' Favorite Author and later inducted into Heartsong's Hall of Fame. Several of her books have appeared on the CBA bestseller list.

Books by Colleen L. Reece

HEARTSONG PRESENTS

Don't miss out on any of our super romances. Write to us at the following address for information on our newest releases and club information.

Heartsong Presents Readers' Service
PO Box 721
Uhrichsville, OH 44683

Or visit www.heartsongpresents.com

Romance Rides the Range

Colleen L. Reece

Heartsong Presents

For Susan K. Marlow, author of the Circle C Adventures series—who not only insisted I write this book but took me to California to research it!

Gratefully,
Colleen

A note from the Author:
I love to hear from my readers! You may correspond with me by writing:

Colleen L. Reece
Author Relations
PO Box 721
Uhrichsville, OH 44683

ISBN 978-1-60260-895-5

ROMANCE RIDES THE RANGE

Our mission is to publish and distribute inspirational products offering exceptional value and biblical encouragement to the masses.

PRINTED IN THE U.S.A.

one

"It's over, girl. Git up." Gus Stoddard's gruff voice crackled with impatience.

Seventeen-year-old Sarah Joy Anderson ignored the command and continued to bend over the freshly dug grave. Her tears fell freely, mixing with the recent rain shower. The April morning's sudden cloudburst symbolized her grief. It was as if all heaven wept on her behalf. The shower had cleared the air of the usual humidity of the St. Louis, Missouri, day and left the morning refreshingly cool and clean. A rainbow spread its half circle over her mother's grave just as the minister read John 14:1–3—a fitting eulogy for a God-fearing woman like Virginia Anderson Stoddard.

" 'Let not your heart be troubled: ye believe in God, believe also in me. In my Father's house are many mansions: if it were not so, I would have told you. I go to prepare a place for you. And if I go and prepare a place for you, I will come again, and receive you unto myself; that where I am, there ye may be also.' "

The familiar words brought a measure of comfort, but it fled like darkness from dawn at her stepfather's harsh voice.

"I said git up, girl." This time, the hard prod of a leather boot accompanied Gus's voice. "The young-uns are hungry. You take 'em back to the house and fix 'em some dinner. I've got business down at the docks."

A wave of rebellion swept through Sarah. "I want to stay here awhile."

"It doesn't matter what you want. Do as I say. Now." Gus yanked Sarah up from the mound of dirt. He spun her around so hard her worn bonnet slipped to her shoulders, revealing a thick braid of red gold hair circling her head. "Look at you. There's no call to shame yourself in front of the preacher and mourners by crawling all over the grave. You've got mud on your Sunday-go-to-meeting dress. You're a disgrace! What would your mother think of you wallowing in the mud instead of minding your brothers and sister?"

They are no kin of mine, Sarah silently protested. Long experience with Gus Stoddard had taught her to hold her tongue even when she wanted to cry out against him.

Sarah glanced down through tears at her blue-sprigged calico dress. Several large, dark splotches covered the skirt and the undersides of the long sleeves. Her hands were caked with mud from falling onto the mound of dirt that held the last remains of the dearest person she'd ever known. *Oh Mama. What will become of me now?* She read the tombstone once more: VIRGINIA STODDARD. 1840–82. Nothing more. No words of endearment, no mention of the other little life that lay in the woman's arms—the tiny baby girl who had never even been named. Engraving cost money—more than the unfeeling man standing next to Sarah cared to pay. He certainly wouldn't see the need to write anything other than the bare-bone facts.

Sarah looked up and blinked back tears. Most of the twenty-five or so mourners had gone, leaving her alone with the man who now had control over her life. She gazed silently into Gus Stoddard's face. It seemed chiseled from stone. The hard black eyes staring at her from beneath heavy brows made Sarah wonder what her gentle mother had ever seen in this man.

Perhaps Gus had been handsome at one time, with his thick, curling dark hair and solid muscular build. Sadly, whatever charms he'd used to win Virginia Anderson had quickly worn off after the marriage vows. It had been the longest three years of Sarah's life.

"What are you staring at, girl?" Gus demanded, giving her a hard shake.

She fought back fear and revulsion. "Nothing." Her voice was so devoid of emotion it earned her a sharp smack across the cheek. She ignored the slap as she had learned to ignore so many things from her stepfather.

"Mind your impertinence, missy," Gus snapped. "We can't stand around all day grieving over a dead woman. There's work t'be done, you hear? Take your brothers and sister home while I mosey down to the docks. I've got business with Tice Edwards."

The look on Gus's face convinced Sarah he was in no mood to be trifled with. She grabbed eight-year-old Ellianna by the hand. "Come on. Let's go home." With her other hand she reached for five-year-old Timmy and motioned for the two older boys to follow. Together they headed back to the three-room cottage on the edge of town, the Stoddards' most recent residence. It was a two-mile hike through the bustling city of St. Louis; the humidity that had for a short time relented would soon be back in full force.

You're not my pa. Sarah shouted silently. *These are not my brothers and sister.* She gave Ellie's hand an impatient tug. "You're always dragging your feet, Ellie. Can't you walk a little faster? Timmy doesn't have any trouble keeping up."

In response, the child bit Sarah's hand.

"Ouch!" Sarah yelped. "What did you do that for?"

"You were pulling too hard," Ellie answered spitefully, glancing at the older boys walking alongside. They grinned.

Ian, the oldest at thirteen, stopped and shoved his hands into his pockets. "I ain't goin' home," he announced, kicking at a rock with one bare foot. "I'm goin' t'catch me some rats down by the riverboats."

"I'm goin', too," declared eleven-year-old Peter. He pulled back on his suspenders and let them go, grinning at the loud crack they made.

"Fine," Sarah muttered. "The rest of us are going home for nice hot stew and my special biscuits. You two aren't getting any if you don't come now."

The older boys looked at each other. Ian shrugged his shoulders then turned and took off toward the docks. Peter glanced briefly at Sarah then hurried after his brother.

The two youngest children whined and kicked. "We wanna go, too!"

Sarah held firmly to their arms. "You'll fall into the river and drown; then where will I be?" she growled over their screams of rage. "Just settle down and come along."

When they finally reached home, the need to heat yesterday's stew and mix up a batch of biscuits pushed Sarah's grief to the back of her mind for a few minutes. But as she pulled the hot pan from the small, black beast of a cookstove, the familiar odor of her mother's baking powder biscuits wafted on the air and set Sarah to crying again. She dropped the pan on the top of the stove, hastily dished up the stew, and placed the food before the two hungry children. They instantly set to eating with fingers and spoons.

"You're welcome," Sarah muttered past the lump in her throat. She untied her apron, hung it on a nail, and headed for the ladder to the loft she shared with Ellie and the boys. A thin blanket hanging from a tightly stretched rope separated the attic into two rooms. Sarah pushed past the flimsy partition and flung herself down on her corn-husk mattress, sobbing.

Why had God taken Mama and the newborn baby?

When no more tears came, Sarah rolled over and stared at the attic ceiling. The pine boards were old and warped. Here and there a chink of sunlight showed through the tar paper and rough shake roof. Was there any hope it would be repaired before fall? *Hardly.* Gus Stoddard was not long on work. He could usually be found doing the least strenuous job for the most money. Gambling figured highly in his income opportunities, but Sarah knew he lost far more money than he won. She only had to look around the cramped shack and count the number of times she mended britches and lowered hems to figure out Gus was just as poor at gambling as he was at any honest venture. When things got too lean, he'd find work on the docks just long enough to tide them over for a few weeks.

"Oh God!" Sarah cried out to the ceiling. "Why did You let Mama die? How will I get along without her?" A vision of what lay ahead sent a cold chill into the girl's aching heart. Virginia had named her only daughter Sarah Joy, but what little joy Sarah had known during the past three years was buried in a lonely grave.

Thinking about her mother's death plunged Sarah into the past—to the tragic death of her father five years before: the lingering illness that transformed the tall, strong but gentle Scandinavian giant into a thin, pale shadow. The anguish of watching their once-productive farm slowly deteriorate into disrepair when John Anderson could no longer work it. The final, agonizing hours of a wonderful husband and father. Although he had no fear of death, he mourned for his family, who would soon be left alone in the world. Seeing him so had wrenched Sarah's heart but not like this most recent, terrible loss. Now she was alone. Alone with—

"Why did you have to marry that horrible Gus Stoddard?"

she sobbed. "We were getting along all right. You, Seth, and me." Even as she spoke, Sarah knew it wasn't quite true. Although her brother, Seth, had worked hard, he couldn't make the farm pay. Forced to sell Pleasant Acres, the family relocated to St. Louis, but every day was a struggle to live.

A year later Virginia Anderson had informed her eighteen-year-old son and thirteen-year-old daughter that she was remarrying. "He's a widower," she said. "A kind, God-fearing Christian man I met at a church social. He has four motherless children. The youngest is only two years old. Mr. Stoddard is anxious to share his home with a woman who will treat his children as her own. In exchange he will make a good husband and provide a home for us."

Sarah snorted. "A good husband?" she said disgustedly. She pulled herself to a sitting position on her bed, clenched her fists, and savagely slammed them onto her thin, uncomfortable mattress. Gus Stoddard had been desperate for a woman. A woman who would do all the work without even a thank-you. A woman who would care for his unruly, disrespectful children and go for days wondering when her new husband would return from his many "business" deals.

"Translation," Sarah sneered, "gambling and drinking binges. We were better off starving to death by ourselves."

She closed her eyes and tried to shove the pain of the last three years from her mind. "It's over," she insisted. "No point in digging up old memories. They should stay buried. I've got enough trouble right now without borrowing from the past." *"Sufficient unto the day is the evil thereof."* The verse from Matthew's Gospel popped into her head, but it did little to quiet her anxiety. Sarah knew the verse referred to worrying about tomorrow, but was God also trying to tell her to let the past take care of itself?

It was no use. Memories flooded her troubled mind, and

Sarah could do nothing to stop them. At last she gave in and relived the heart-wrenching weeks that had followed her mother's marriage to Gus.

ঌ

Sarah and her brother saw through their new stepfather immediately. Gus Stoddard proved himself a hypocrite from the honeymoon on. Not once did he step into a church after the marriage ceremony. He dragged Seth to the docks to work, beating him if he raised the slightest objection. He forced Sarah to accept work as a laundress. Her hands turned raw and bled. Did she or Seth see a penny of their wages? Of course not! Gus pocketed the money then gambled it away.

A year later Seth made a bold move. "I'm going west," he confided to his sister one spring evening near the back fence. "I can't take old man Stoddard one day longer." Seth squared his shoulders, and a parting ray of sunlight rested on the red gold hair that matched his sister's. His once-laughing mouth tightened into a straight line. With a pang, Sarah realized the childhood companion she adored was now a man. A man like their father, who had set his course and would not deviate from it.

"What about. . .what about Mama. . .and me?" Sarah asked, frightened. Seth leave? Unthinkable! Who'd stand between her and Gus when the disreputable man had had too much to drink and started on a rampage?

two

Seth looked troubled. His blue eyes, so like Sarah's, darkened in concern. "I talked to Mama," he assured her. "She agrees it's best for me to leave. Gus is bound and determined to apprentice me to some wheelwright or blacksmith. Even worse, he wants me to learn the gambling trade." Seth laughed bitterly. "What do you think our pa would say about that?"

Sarah shook her head. "Pa never gambled a day in his life. Nor drank a drop of whiskey. He loved God and Mother. And us." Her voice quavered. "Seth, what will become of Mama and me?"

He reached out and pulled his young sister close. "Never you mind. Just hang on for a year or two. I'll go west and become a cowboy. I've heard they don't make much money, but if you're good at your job, you can get steady work all year round." He paused and added softly, "I'll pray every day for God to watch over you until I can save enough to send for you and Mama."

Sarah shook her head. "You know Mama won't leave Gus and the kids. She made a promise, remember? 'In sickness and in health. Till death do us part.' Just like she promised Pa. Mama will honor her vows—even if it costs her everything." A sob rose in her throat, but she hastily swallowed it. Seth *had* to go. She must not make it harder for him than she knew it already was.

"All right then. I'll send for *you*, little sister."

Sarah felt her heart leap with sudden hope. To be free of her brutal stepfather would be the greatest gift her brother could give her. Just as quickly her joy vanished and a dull ache entered her heart. *How can I leave? Mama relies on me for more than just help in managing the house. The kids don't listen—they make more work for her. Who would she talk with in the long evenings when Gus is gone? I'm Mama's only confidante. God, I simply can't leave her.*

Sarah felt torn in two. She loved her mother, yet she adored her brother. Since their father's death, Seth had been her protector, her cherished companion, her safeguard against some of her stepfather's unpredictable moods. More than once Gus's upraised hand had been stayed because of Seth's presence. What would happen when her brother left? She shuddered. She dared not remind Seth of this, or he might stay on her account. That must not happen. Although Gus held back from brutalizing the women, he clearly had no qualms about laying into Seth for the smallest offense. One of these days the beast would beat Seth senseless—or kill him in a drunken rage.

Sarah sighed, her decision made. "I can't leave, I'll get by." She clasped one of Seth's hands. "But you're right. You've got to leave before our stepfather does something terrible to you. He's a mean one. Stubborn, too. He'll no doubt have the law after you, seeing you're not yet of age. If you can only stay out of his clutches for two years, you'll be safe."

Seth heaved a sigh. "I know. I don't want to leave you and Mama, but I've got her blessing. She gave me what money she could spare. It must mean the Lord's going to look after me."

"I hope so, Seth." Sarah gave her brother a hug. "Write to us, would you? Let us know where you are."

"I'll try. But it'll probably be some time before I settle down in one place long enough to write."

"When are you leaving?"

"Right away." His face gleamed in the growing dusk. "I

already said good-bye to Mama. Gus is down at the docks, hanging around his favorite riverboat. He'll no doubt be gone all night. By the time he staggers home, I'll be long gone." Seth paused then quickly added, "Thank God that for once in their marriage Mama stood up to Gus when he wanted to sell Copper! I wouldn't get far on foot. Even so, I can only carry food and a few extras in the saddlebags. Look after what little else I have, won't you, and bring it when you come."

He paused. "Don't worry if you don't hear from me for a while. When I do write, I'll send the letters to. . ." He named a trusted friend. "We can't take a chance on Gus intercepting them."

Sarah sadly nodded and watched her brother walk off into the night. The sound of creaking leather, followed by the soft *thud* of the sorrel's hooves diminished, leaving her alone in the darkness. Hot tears fell as she hurried to hide her brother's few pitiful childhood treasures. The Stoddard children mustn't get their greedy little hands on Seth's belongings, especially the toy pistol Seth's pa had painstakingly carved for him years before, so perfect in detail it closely resembled the real thing.

&

Days passed. Gus Stoddard's initial fury at Seth's departure waned. A muttered "good riddance" a few weeks later assured Sarah and her mother that he had no immediate plans to track the young man down and drag him home. Life settled into routine—an empty routine for Sarah, who missed Seth's hearty laugh and reassuring presence more than she had dreamed possible.

Months limped by with no news of Seth. Sarah feared some misfortune had befallen her brother in the wild West. Each night after the youngsters had been put to bed, Sarah and her mother fell to their knees, asking God to keep His strong hand upon Seth. They also prayed for a letter.

More than a year later the longed-for missive finally arrived, delivered by Seth's friend. Seth was safe! Sarah and her mother rejoiced but kept the news to themselves, hiding the letter long before Gus returned from spending most of the afternoon and evening gambling away the little money he had. It would do Seth no good for Gus to learn the young man was now in California.

Seth had written that he loved learning the cowboy trade on the Diamond S Ranch. "I'm the greenest greenhorn in the entire outfit," he lamented in his letter. "I don't know why my boss, Matt Sterling, has taken such a shine to me, but if it weren't for him, I'd probably be lying dead in some back alley in Madera." He closed his letter by writing, "Don't worry. I'm alive, I've got a good job, and I am saving all I can. Keep praying for me. I know it's those prayers that have seen me through some hard times."

Other letters arrived, secretly delivered by Seth's friend. Usually they were short, with just bits and pieces of news about Seth's new life. He loved the mild climate and the opportunity to make something of himself by working hard. He was happy, Sarah could tell. She only wished—

&

A crash and a piercing scream jerked Sarah abruptly from her musing. She leaped from the mattress and scrambled down the ladder. Ellie and Timmy were at each other's throats—biting, pinching, and hitting. Timmy was crying; Ellie shrieked at the top of her lungs.

"Stop that at once!" Sarah ordered, grasping the back of Timmy's overalls. She gave a yank, which forced the little boy to let go of his sister. "What's going on?"

Ellie threw herself at Timmy. Sarah had all she could do to avoid the child's flailing fists. "He stole it!" Ellie screamed. "Give it back, you crybaby!"

Timmy howled. "She's killin' me, Sarah! Make her stop!"

Just then the door to the cottage burst open. Ian and Peter strolled through—dirty and rumpled. They whooped in delight at the scuffle but made no move to aid Sarah. Instead they watched from the doorway as their stepsister fought to control the two children.

"You two give me a hand here," she ordered the boys.

"We're hungry," Peter answered, ignoring her request. He and Ian grinned, stepped around the ruckus, and began opening and closing cupboards in search of something to eat.

Ellie and Timmy screamed louder. Sarah held them at arm's length and tried to make them hush. A swift kick from the little girl sent a chair tumbling over.

"Can't a man return to his home without finding it in an uproar?" A bellow from behind Sarah sliced through the commotion.

Silence fell. Sarah released the children. They turned to stare at Gus Stoddard and a dark-haired, dark-eyed stranger standing in the open doorway of their tiny cottage.

"Here I am bringing a guest home and what greets us?" Gus roared. "A barroom brawl! Shame on you all." He turned and focused most of his wrath on Sarah. "You, Sarah. You're a grown woman. I expect you to keep these kids under control." He waved an arm toward the cluttered room that served as both the kitchen and sitting room. "Look at this mess. You've let it fall apart the past couple of weeks. Rubbish everywhere." He kicked at an empty whiskey bottle. "You're to be keeping the place clean, girl. I've told you time and time again."

Sarah felt her cheeks flame in red-hot anger. *Keep this place clean? How dare you!* She wanted to shout into his face that it was he and his disheveled pack of rowdy youngsters who turned this tiny shack into a garbage heap most days. If Mama hadn't worked so hard that she collapsed a few days before the baby came, perhaps both of them wouldn't have died in childbirth. Sarah had been too overwhelmed with trying to care for her dying mother to keep the place straightened up.

Gus glowered at her and continued his rampage. He waggled a finger in her face. "You, m'girl, are not making a very good impression on Mr. Edwards. I told him you kept a tidy house."

Sarah shoved her anger to a corner of her mind and shifted her gaze from her stepfather to the stranger. So this was Tice Edwards, with whom her stepfather did business. An older man, but not as old as Gus, he stood tall and proud, with coal-black hair cut short and slicked back. No ragged beard or mustache marred his chiseled face. Above a straight nose, his dark eyes gleamed with interest and amusement. When he caught Sarah's appraising look, he nodded slightly. "Good evening." His words were refined, silky, polished, but his bold stare made Sarah squirm.

She dropped her gaze and stared at a crack in the floor, mind awhirl. Just who was this obviously wealthy and high-class Tice Edwards? Certainly not one of Gus's usual companions. Many a night Sarah and her mother had been forced to endure the company of rowdy and ill-mannered guests crowded into the house, but Mr. Edwards had never been part of those gatherings. Whatever did he see in her stepfather?

While she was still trying to piece together the significance of Mr. Edwards's unexpected visit, Gus strode across the room, draped a heavy, dirty arm across Sarah's shoulders and grinned at his guest. The matter of the filthy cabin suddenly seemed insignificant. "So, what do you think of her, Tice? We sort of caught my daughter unawares, and I know she ain't dressed for company, but you can see she's a real looker. Think she'll do?"

Sarah flinched at her stepfather's touch and twisted free. Her throat went dry. *Do?* What kind of employment was Gus arranging for her *this* time? Scullery maid? Cook? Upstairs maid? Probably not, she reasoned, if the cottage was intended to be a job reference. It really *was* a jumble tonight. Perhaps Mr. Tice Edwards would turn up his nose and stalk out the door in a huff. Judging from appearances, the man could afford many servants. Why would he consider hiring anyone Gus Stoddard put forward? Sarah swallowed and chewed thoughtfully on her lower lip. Perhaps working in a fine home would be a step up from serving as a drudge to Gus.

The next instant she saw the intense, eager look on Tice's face. Sarah decided she did not want to work for him after all—no matter how much he might pay. As unpleasant as her life was with Gus Stoddard, now that her mother was gone, she didn't like the looks of this expensively clad stranger. He stared at her like she was a slab of prime beef hanging in the butcher's window. She couldn't abide the thought of those probing eyes watching her carry out her duties in his home. Sarah steeled herself to refuse his offer of employment.

Tice strolled leisurely across the floor and came to a stop a few inches from where she stood next to Gus. He caught her chin and forced her to meet his gaze. "She'll do nicely." He chuckled. "Needs a bit of cleaning up, but you're right. She's real pretty."

"Then it's a deal?" Gus asked eagerly.

Tice dropped his hand and smiled. Straight, white teeth flashed. A line from a fairy tale crossed Sarah's mind. *"The better to eat you with, my dear."* "It's a deal."

Sarah rubbed her chin and turned on her stepfather. "What's a deal?" she demanded. "If you think I'm going to work for Mr. Edwards, you're mistaken."

Gus's slap sent Sarah reeling. He shot an apologetic look

toward Tice. "She's a mite feisty sometimes, Tice. Didn't have real good bringing up, I'm afraid." He waggled a finger at Sarah. "You're not going to work for Mr. Edwards, m'girl. You're going to be his wife."

three

Sarah staggered to her feet. "His—his—*wife?*" she stuttered, unable to grasp what Gus was saying. The stinging pain of her stepfather's slap went unheeded. She stumbled to the crude table and leaned against it, breathing hard. *This can't be happening. Please, God, let it all be a bad dream.*

Tice Edwards quickly joined Sarah. "If I may?" he offered, pulling out a chair. His silken words flowed over Sarah like sweet, sticky honey.

She shivered and closed her eyes then crumpled into the chair. She buried her head in her arms and fought against the nausea that threatened to overwhelm her. Hot tears sprang to her eyes, but she forced them back. *This is not a crying matter,* Sarah told herself fiercely. *I must think. I must get control of myself.*

A whimper brought Sarah's head up. Timmy stood at the end of the table, biting his lip. His light brown hair curled around his ears and fell into his wide, dark eyes. His hands were thrust into the pockets of his overalls, and he sniffled. When Sarah caught his gaze, he blinked hard and whispered, "Sarah?"

Her heart softened at the uncertainty on the little boy's face. But before she could respond to him, Gus barked, "Get outside—all of you. Don't come in till I tell you."

"I want Sarah," Timmy pleaded. He'd swiftly changed from the screaming, fighting little tiger of a few minutes ago to a scared child in need of a hug. No matter how irritated Sarah found herself at the antics of Gus's children, it was clear

Timmy knew where he could find shelter during his father's many angry storms. He reached for her in spite of his father's order.

"Git, I told you!" Gus took a swipe at Timmy, but the boy was too quick. He ducked under Gus's arm and scampered outdoors with a frightened yelp. The other children had already disappeared through the door, away from their father's rotten temper and heavy hand.

Sarah heard the harsh teasing of the older boys and Timmy's sobbing through the open door. She clenched her fists. She wanted to rush outside and gather Timmy into her arms. Of Gus's four children, Timmy was the sensitive one, the child who had known Sarah's mother as his only mother and Sarah as his real sister. When he wasn't being influenced for evil by his older siblings, he was a loving little boy.

The brush of Tice's hand across the braid on the top of Sarah's head brought her around. She shook herself free of his touch and stood. She looked up, gripped the edge of the table to steady herself, and took a deep breath. Ice tinkled in her voice as she said, "I will not marry you, Mr. Edwards."

Gus lurched forward, hand raised, but Tice motioned him away with a curt wave. "No more of that, Gus. I don't want my future wife marred for her wedding day." He gave Sarah a rueful smile. "I'm sorry the arrangements are not to your liking, Miss Stoddard—"

"*Anderson*," Sarah corrected between clenched teeth.

Tice bowed. "My mistake, Miss Anderson. I apologize. I regret I haven't made a good impression on you, but contrary to what your stepfather told you earlier, you *have* made a good first impression on me." He grinned. "Actually, a second impression."

Sarah's stomach lurched. "I've never seen you before. How could I have made any impression on you?"

"You'd better explain it to her, Gus," Tice suggested quietly. He waved toward the chair Sarah had recently vacated. "Please sit down."

Sarah sat. Her palms turned clammy. She rubbed them against her skirt and then clenched them in her lap. She kept her expression stony when she turned to face her stepfather, dreading and fearing what he would say.

Gus sauntered over to the cookstove and peered into the speckled enamel coffeepot. He grunted, poured himself a cup of the steaming brew, crossed the room, and plunked himself down into an overstuffed armchair that had seen better days. "Well now, Sarah, the truth of the matter is this: My friend Tice has had his eye on you for quite some time. He saw you one day down by the docks and decided you were the girl for him. O'course, that was a few years back, but I promised I'd make arrangements for your—*betrothal*—as soon as an opportunity presented itself." He paused and looked at her over the rim of his coffee cup.

Sarah saw in Gus's steely eyes the truth of the past three years. He had used her mother from the very beginning— used her as nothing more than a slave. He had run her ragged taking care of his four kids and trying to keep everyone fed. He took, took, took and never returned a shred of decency, never regarded Virginia Anderson Stoddard as the companion and confidante that God intended a wife should be to her husband. Now Gus planned to use her, too. But why would he be willing to have her marry Tice and leave his children without anyone to care for them?

An ugly thought sprang to life in Sarah's head, and she leaped to her feet. *Money. It's got to have something to do with money.*

Disgust permeated her. It blotted out fear. Slow, hot rage slowly worked its way from the pit of her belly to the roots of her strawberry blond, braided coronet. "You waited until my mother died," she lashed out in sudden realization. "She never would have stood for this, you—you—*swine*; I despise you!"

Sarah's outburst brought a bark of laughter from Tice. "Yes sir, Gus. I like her. She's got spirit. I've had more than my share of clinging, simpering females over the years. Your girl will be a welcome diversion. I'll be proud to stroll with her along the deck of the *River Queen* and show her off to all those luckless gentlemen who missed such a catch."

The gumption inherited from her strong Scandinavian father now served her in good stead. She drew herself up to her full five-feet, four-inch height, raised her chin, and slowly paid out words like a miser pays out gold. "I already told you, Mr. Edwards: I will not marry you—*ever*." Sarah felt stronger now. Her angry response to Gus had helped her gather her wits and prepare for battle. It *was* a battle—one she dared not lose. She took a few steps toward the ladder that led to her attic sanctuary. "If you will excuse me, I'm tired." She nodded at Tice. "I could say it was a pleasure meeting you, Mr. Edwards, but it wasn't. Good evening."

Gus lurched from his chair and hurled his half-empty coffee cup across the room. It slammed into the ladder steps, inches from Sarah's face. Dark brown liquid splattered her skirt. She froze. "You stay put and hear us out, girl." Gus's eyes blazed. "Your playacting and putting on fancy airs won't get you anywhere." He caught Sarah by the wrist and gave it a painful twist.

"Gus," Tice protested, "that's enough."

Gus ignored the warning. With a practiced hand he maneuvered Sarah toward the overstuffed chair and forced her to sit. Then he shook a bony finger in her face. "The fact is, missy, you've belonged to Tice Edwards for some time," he gloated. "Your signature on the marriage papers is all that remains to make it legal."

Sarah opened her mouth to protest, but the sudden, desperate look on Gus's face made her close it again.

"Perhaps I should continue, Gus," Tice broke in. "Miss Anderson, you are overwrought." He crossed the room and knelt down beside the armchair. "You must forgive your stepfather, Sarah, my dear. He's been under quite a strain the past two years. Gus owes me money—a *lot* of money. He's accumulated quite a gambling debt aboard the *River Queen*. I should have tossed him overboard long ago, but. . ." He allowed his gaze to linger on Sarah's face. "He assured me his collateral was worth allowing him a chance to win his losses back." Tice sighed. "Unfortunately Gus is not an especially good gambler. His losses keep piling up. The good news is that when you become my wife, I will cancel all debts against him. In addition, as my father-in-law, he will have the privilege of gambling as often and for as much as he likes aboard the *Queen*. Your brothers and sister need never worry about going hungry again." He grinned. "They could stay on board ship if they liked."

"They're not my brothers and sister," Sarah choked out. It was a stupid thing to say. But she could think of nothing else—not while her heart was slamming against her chest like a mighty fist and her stomach threatened to empty itself. The look in Tice Edwards's eyes reminded her of a reptile's eyes, a reptile waiting to strike its prey.

Tice smiled and patted her hand. "You may leave the children here, if you wish. It is immaterial to me *where* they live, my dear."

Sarah snatched her hand away and sent a shriveling glance at her stepfather. "This can't be legal. You can't force me to marry this—this—*snake*! I'll go to the police. I'll tell them, tell them—"

"Tell them what, Sarah?" Tice stood and smiled down at her. "That your *legal guardian*—under whose authority you must remain until you are eighteen years of age—has made a perfectly good marriage contract for you? I am more than qualified for the position of a caring husband. I can provide not only for you but also for your entire family. I am one of the most prominent men of this city. The police would laugh at your foolish talk and send you home." Tice grinned. "Trust me. I know. The chief of police is one of my regulars aboard the *Queen*."

Sarah ignored his remarks and focused on what he'd said earlier. "What do you mean, my *legal guardian*? That's rubbish. My real father is dead, and Gus is nothing more than a poor excuse for a stand-in."

Tice raised a sardonic eyebrow. "An attorney friend of mine and I helped arrange the matter of guardianship papers a little over a year ago." He turned to Gus. "You never told her?"

"Must've slipped my mind." Gus ambled over to the cookstove and poured himself a second cup of coffee. Then he looked at Sarah and smirked. "Sorry."

Sarah tried to absorb this new and unwelcome news. It was no use. Instead she did what she had promised herself she would not do in front of these men—she curled into a small ball in the depths of the armchair and burst into uncontrollable sobs.

When no more tears fell, Sarah rubbed her eyes and looked around. The cabin lay empty and quiet. She heard nothing except an occasional cockroach skittering across the wooden floor on its nightly round of foraging. The three small lamps that provided light burned low, casting the room into deep shadows. Sarah shivered. Where was Gus? Where were the children?

"Who cares?" she said, rising from the chair. For the first

time since her mother had taken sick, Sarah was alone in the cottage. She crossed to the stove and checked the fire. Several coals still burned a dull red. Sarah quickly tossed a few sticks of firewood onto the bed of coals, fanned them to life, and slammed the door shut. She settled the coffeepot over the hottest spot, opened the lid, and peeked inside. There was enough for another cup. Good! She needed a hot, strong cup of coffee to sharpen her wits.

Her stomach rumbled, and Sarah remembered she'd eaten nothing since breakfast. She glanced over at the crude table, but not one biscuit remained of the batch she'd made for Timmy and Ellie. Had it been only a few short hours ago that she'd tossed the food on the table and fled to her attic refuge? It seemed like a century since she'd bade her mother good-bye that morning. Nothing seemed real. How could her life suddenly turn so much worse in just one day? She'd thought there could be no more terrible fate than drudging for Gus. Now she knew better. Being married to a man she did not love, a man like Tice Edwards, was even worse than being a servant in her stepfather's house. *Infinitely worse!*

four

All Sarah's dreams of what she imagined the perfect marriage would be came from her own parents' life together. She couldn't have had a better example. Her father and mother had honored and respected as well as loved each other. Sarah, even in the earliest stages of budding womanhood, recognized how important that was in a godly marriage. She thrilled when she caught the look that sometimes passed between her mother and father as they shared a secret joke or wanted to communicate without letting Seth and Sarah know. It was like magic, Sarah realized. It had made such a deep impression that she vowed never to give her life into another's keeping until God sent someone of His own choosing—and she looked forward to the time when she and her future husband would share such special moments.

An overheard conversation had deepened Sarah's determination. One bright summer morning Sarah had started lightly down the stairs of the farmhouse where she had been born. Halfway down she heard voices from the parlor. Mama had a caller. Sarah sighed and cast a longing look out the open screen door into the lovely, beckoning day. If Mama heard her, she'd be summoned into the parlor and forced to be polite to some tiresome neighbor.

Sarah turned to tiptoe back upstairs but froze when she heard a recently married young woman, scarcely more than a girl, say, "Mrs. Anderson—Virginia—everyone knows what a wonderful marriage you have. I want to work hard to have the same. I know a lot of it is because you are both strong

Christians, but there must be something more. Please. Tell me your secret to finding happiness."

The unseen eavesdropper held her breath, waiting for her mother's reply. After a low, amused laugh, Virginia Anderson's voice rang like a silver bell. "Letty, John and I have always been so busy making sure the other person is happy that we haven't needed to 'find happiness,' as you put it. It's just there. In abundance."

Sarah never forgot her mother's simple recipe for joy in marriage. The words sank into her pounding heart and glowed like a precious gem.

Now, years later, Sarah mourned while she rummaged through the cupboards for something to fill her stomach. "This can't be happening. I cannot, *will not* marry Tice Edwards. I don't even know him. Why would such a man want to marry me in the first place? He doesn't know me. How could he just up and decide he wants me based on one or two stingy little glimpses? It's absurd!"

Sarah slammed the cupboard door shut and stepped to the stove to pour a cup of warmed-over coffee. With a tired sigh she settled herself at the table and pondered her situation. She wanted a husband with whom she could laugh, enjoy life, and confide. One who would put God first and lead his family in Bible readings and evening prayers. "It wouldn't hurt if he was a hardworking man like Pa," she added, sipping the bitter brew. She made a face. "Maybe I'm expecting too much. Maybe they're all like Gus. At least the boys and men from around here are all cut from the same bolt of burlap— rough and ugly."

The image of two men instantly came to mind: her brother Seth, no longer troubled-looking but smiling at her from a faded photograph he'd sent in one of his rare letters, and the tall, dark-haired stranger posing beside him. A rough-clad stranger whose steady gaze and half smile reassured Sarah that her brother had found a true friend. Her heartbeat quickened. "I'll bet he isn't like Gus," she whispered. "Matthew Sterling looks kind and good. According to Seth, he's as solid and true as his name."

She closed her eyes and imagined the stranger riding up to rescue her from the unspeakable future Gus and Tice planned. The next instant Sarah shook her head. "Appearances are just that—appearances. Seth might be mistaken about his friend. Even though Matthew means *gift of the Lord,* he might be no better than Gus and Tice."

Sarah sighed. If all men were like those two, she would *never* marry. Better to live alone than live married to someone she didn't love—or worse, who would never really love her the way God meant a husband to love his wife.

"So, God, what am I supposed to do?" she pleaded. "Tice Edwards is obviously a man used to getting his own way. He's no doubt got a justice or a preacher or two under his thumb. How am I going to escape this trap they've laid for me?" She took another gulp of coffee and stared at the tabletop.

Like a gentle breeze a scripture verse whispered in her mind. *"There hath no temptation taken you but such as is common to man: but God is faithful, who will not suffer you to be tempted above that ye are able; but will with the temptation also make a way to escape, that ye may be able to bear it."*

Escape? Yes! Sarah's heartbeat quickened. She must flee from the fate Gus intended for her. But how? Gus was clearly trapped in Tice's web of debt as surely as they intended to trap Sarah. "Perhaps there's a different way," she murmured. "If I could offer Gus another way out of his debt, he might not be so keen on marrying me off." She managed a small smile of hope. Maybe Gus could ask Tice Edwards to extend the loan one more time. If he—

The door swung open and smashed against the wall in the middle of Sarah's musings. Timmy entered first. He ran to Sarah and threw his thin little arms around her neck. The other boys shuffled past and plopped themselves on the floor in the center of the room with a pack of playing cards. Ellie sat down at the table near Sarah and just looked at her. As usual nobody said a word. No one offered an explanation of their recent whereabouts.

Sarah sighed. Keeping track of the Stoddard children was worse than trying to corral a flock of frightened chickens. The only relief she got was the days they were in school and she had the house to herself. Some days the older boys played hooky and surprised her by crashing in through the door and upsetting all her carefully laid plans.

Gus burst in and kicked the door shut with the heel of his boot. He lifted a bottle filled with amber liquid to his lips and took a swallow. "Well, Sarah," he drawled, "I gave you a few minutes by yourself to work things through." He fell into the ragged armchair and waited.

If Gus thinks I'll thank him for this small consideration, he is greatly mistaken, Sarah decided. Just looking at him made the bile rise in her throat. She swallowed hard and determined to work on an escape plan right away. "I'm not going to marry Tice," she stated. Before Gus could strike out, Sarah continued. "Promise you won't force me to marry Mr. Edwards, and I'll pay off the debt you owe him. I'll find work—good-paying work—and I'll pay back every cent. I'll keep this place clean and care for the kids. Just don't make me marry him."

Gus grinned and took a swallow of whiskey. "Sarah, Sarah." He chuckled softly, shaking his head. "You are such an innocent. Have you any idea how much I owe Tice Edwards?"

She shook her head.

"I owe him more than six thousand dollars."

Sarah blanched. "Six thousand dollars?" If she worked day and night until she was an old woman, she could never hope to pay back such a sum. Her hopes crashed. In desperation she threw herself to the floor in front of Gus. "Please," she pleaded, "don't force me to marry Mr. Edwards. Who will take care of the children if I'm gone? Timmy's still little. Ellie's too young to look after him all day while you're out of the house."

"Who'd take care of 'em if you hired yourself out to work?" Gus growled. He sat up and leaned closer to his stepdaughter. "I can get me another woman anytime I want. Just like I got your ma. It ain't hard to do. Your ma is proof of that."

It took every ounce of self-control Sarah had to keep from grabbing a frying pan off the dilapidated stove and giving him a whack. How could he speak that way, with Mama barely cold in the grave?

Gus reached out and grasped Sarah's wrist. "I'll tell you another thing, missy. Tice Edwards sees something in you he likes. I don't know what, but you'll not do anything to make him change his mind, you hear? He's a gentleman. Told me he plans to court you right and proper for a week or two—starting tomorrow. You'd best get yourself cleaned up and ready when he comes calling in the afternoon. Or else." He thrust her aside and went back to his bottle. Soon he was snoring loudly, sprawled across the chair with his head thrown back.

Tiptoeing so as not to wake his father, Timmy crept to Sarah and whispered, "I'm hungry."

"It's too late to fix you anything," Sarah muttered, getting up. She turned to Ian and Peter. "Go up to bed, boys. The night's half over."

Ian glared at her while Peter remarked, "We don't have to."

"Fine. Stay up all night. See if I care." Wearily she took

Timmy's hand and glanced around the room for Ellie. The little girl lay sound asleep in a corner, curled into a small, tattered ball. Wisps of dark brown hair fell across her face, pouting even in sleep. Sarah thought about rousing her, but what was the point? Ellie would certainly protest against being wakened and dragged up to the attic. Why care if the child spent the night on the cold, hard floor?

A sliver of guilt stabbed Sarah as she guided Timmy up the steep ladder to the room above. Her mother never would have allowed Ellie to huddle in the corner. Virginia always had a tender word for the fractious little girl, no matter how weary and heartsore she felt after a long day's work.

"I'm not like you, Mama," Sarah confessed in a whisper, giving Timmy one last boost onto the attic floor. "I can't be patient and kind to these rowdy youngsters when my own world is falling apart. I'm sorry."

"What did you say, Sarah?" Timmy asked quietly.

"Never you mind." She tumbled him onto his pallet and tucked the quilt around his peaked face. She rose. "You just go to sleep. It's late."

"Sarah?"

"What now?" Sarah snapped.

"You—you ain't leavin' us to marry that gambler fellow, are you?"

Sarah caught her breath at the fear she heard in Timmy's voice. Reaching down, she patted him on the leg. "I don't know, Timmy. I hope not. But it's nothing you have to worry about right now."

Before he could reply, Sarah crept around the partition and onto her own mattress. The corn husks rustled and crackled while she tried to find a comfortable position for her weary body. Soon she lay still. The rustling ceased. Only the soft laughter of the boys downstairs and the occasional snore of a drunken Gus Stoddard floated up through the hole in the ceiling.

Although Sarah's body was at last at rest, her mind was spinning. The verse from Corinthians about escaping temptation repeated itself in her mind. Her escape from Tice Edwards by offering to pay Gus's debt was obviously not a viable plan. There must be another way to escape.

A familiar verse from Genesis 12 popped into her head. *"Get thee out of thy country, and from thy kindred, and from thy father's house, unto a land that I will shew thee."*

Leave? Sarah held her breath and stared at the pale moonlight peeking through the cracks in the attic roof. *Run away?* She shivered in the dark. How could she just up and leave? She had no place to go, no money to get there. Worse, she would be alone—dreadfully alone.

"Lo, I am with you always, even unto the end of the world."

Sarah held her breath in wonder. All those Bible verses she'd learned as a child were coming back to her just when she needed them most. But again, the word *how* kept rearing its ugly head—mocking her, urging her to stay and accept her future. She wavered. In spite of her unspoken vows never to marry until she felt God approved, maybe marrying Tice Edwards wouldn't be as bad as she was making it out to be. He was rich. He seemed polite and was obviously interested in her. He had spoken gently to her and prevented Gus from striking her.

She chewed on her lip in deep thought and rolled onto her side. The corn husks rustled loudly. There would be no corn husk mattress waiting for her if she married Tice. Only silks and satins. Soft, smooth bedcoverings. No leaking roof. Then, like a clap of thunder, the memory of her mother's marriage to Gus resounded in her memory. Sarah remembered how content her mother had appeared when she knew she was marrying a man who would care for her and for her children. Gus had also seemed the perfect gentleman—before the wedding.

"I can't marry Tice Edwards," Sarah resolved between clenched teeth. "I don't love him. I don't even know him. I must escape. I have no choice." That decided, she gave the situation over to the One who knew exactly what He was doing. "I don't know how I'm going to escape, God, or where I'm going to go," she whispered in the darkness of the attic, "but I do know You're the only One who can help me now. Show me the way." She sighed, turned over, and fell into an uneasy sleep.

five

*Eighteen months earlier
Central California*

Matthew Sterling rode into Madera and dismounted in front of Moore's General Store—which housed the post office—thirsty enough to drain a well. It was over a hundred degrees in the shade, and there was no shade on the ten miles between town and Matt's Diamond S Ranch. Just flat land, dry grass, and a glimpse of the snowcapped Sierra Nevada in the distance, so far away and hazy in the shimmering late September air that the mountains looked like a mirage.

With a practiced flick of his wrist Matt led his favorite buckskin gelding, Chase, to the well-filled horse trough in the middle of town, being careful not to let him drink his fill. "Whoa there," he ordered. "You don't want to founder." He raised his canteen to his own parched lips and grimaced when the lukewarm water poured down his throat.

Matt forced the reluctant horse away from the trough and secured the reins around a nearby hitching rail before giving Chase an affectionate slap on the chest. "Won't be more than a minute, old boy. Gotta pick up the mail, swap a quick 'howdy' with the captain, then it's back to the ranch for a cool drink and some shade." He chuckled as he always did when he thought about stopping by the hotel to greet the captain. He'd known Captain Russell Perry Mace ever since he was a small child, but Matt had never heard the stocky adventurer called anything but *the captain. I guess once a captain, always a captain.*

Even if the Mexican War's been over for ages, Matt thought. Between his title and his ever-present top hat, Captain Mace was an easily recognized figure anywhere in Madera.

Chase shook his dark mane and snorted as if to hurry his master along. He stamped a hoof, and a swirl of pale yellow dust rose up and billowed around the young man.

"Hey!" Matt admonished with a laugh. "None of that. I won't be long." He glanced down at his dust-caked shirt and chaps. What was a little extra dust at this point? He'd been out on the range all day and had built up a good supply of dirt long before Chase showered him.

"Howdy, Matt. Haven't seen you around town for a spell. How're things on the Diamond S?"

Matt turned. Evan Moore, Madera's portly postmaster stood in the doorway of his store grinning. His bald head glistened in the hot afternoon sun. Matt smiled back. "Busy, Evan. Fall roundup's just around the corner."

"Got a full crew?"

"Pretty much. Wish I didn't have to hire on drifters." Matt shook his head and joined the postmaster on the wooden sidewalk. "They're nothing but trouble, but if I don't snatch 'em up, Chapman over at the Redding Ranch is likely to hire 'em. I don't want to be caught shorthanded this year."

"I don't blame you." Evan motioned the young rancher to follow him inside the store. "Don't worry about the dust," he said when Matt removed his wide-brimmed felt hat and slapped it against his chaps before entering. "Can't seem to escape the dust, no matter how hard a body tries. Just like this infernal heat." Evan wiped the sweat from his shining head and strolled to the small cubicle behind the counter that served as the Madera Post Office. He reached into a pigeonhole and withdrew a fistful of envelopes addressed to Matthew Sterling, c/o Diamond S Ranch. "Sorry, Matt. Nothing from Dolores."

"Drat that girl," Matt muttered, swiping at the stubborn hank of black hair that hung over his eyes like a horse's forelock. He replaced his Stetson and sorted through the letters with a scowl. "Don't they teach young ladies to write at that fancy finishing school back east? You'd think Dori could send word to her only brother that she's alive and happy."

The postmaster made no comment.

Matt sighed. He missed little Dori. He missed her chatter. He even missed the silly, affected airs she put on when she wasn't happy with the way things were going out at the ranch. Sending her to school in Boston had been Solita's idea, not his. "Senor Mateo, you must let the senorita finish her education," the diminutive Mexican housekeeper had insisted. "She is unhappy here. Your mama and papa would have allowed it, had they lived. Since they are no longer with us, you must decide what is best for her, not what is best for you."

Matt had agreed, but he wasn't pleased about it. The white stucco, Spanish-style hacienda seemed huge and empty with the only remaining member of his family gone. He enjoyed these rare visits to Madera. Picking up the mail—a task easily done by any greenhorn ranch hand—was Matt's excuse to mingle with the friendly people of the small valley town.

Madera—*lumber* in Spanish—was the perfect name for the thriving little village that had sprung up all at once a few years back. The California Lumber Company had chosen this site along the Southern Pacific Railroad line as the terminus for their timber flume back in 1876. Six months later the town had been laid out, and building had commenced at a lively rate. Matt often paused in the middle of the wide main street to take in the three hotels, three general stores, the drugstore, butcher shop, blacksmith shop, and livery. He thanked God each and every time for timber, flumes, and lumber companies. No longer isolated on his ranch ten miles east of nowhere, the rancher and his hands benefited from the influx of new businesses and the people who ran them. All in all, Madera was—in Matt's opinion—just about the prettiest and most wide-awake town in the entire San Joaquin Valley.

Matt gave Evan a curt good-bye and left the post office in ill humor. It rankled him that Dori, as usual, was probably caught up in her own affairs and wouldn't get around to writing her brother until Christmas. He stuffed the handful of envelopes into his saddlebag and sighed. "Sometimes I wonder why the good Lord made girls in the first place," he muttered. "Trouble. Nothing but trouble."

Matt shook himself free of musings. Thinking about Dori and her irresponsibility invariably made him remember Lydia Hensley. *Forget about her,* he ordered himself, clenching his jaw. *That's over. I'm free of her, and I won't waste the rest of a perfectly good afternoon reflecting on what went wrong between us.*

"Let's get on home, Chase," Matt mumbled to his horse. His trip to town, which he'd looked forward to all day, had turned into a disappointment. Now all he wanted was a bath, a clean set of clothes, and a tall, cool glass of Solita's lemonade—in that order. He untied Chase and glanced toward the elegant, two-story hotel that occupied the best lot in town. "I'll catch the captain later, I guess, though he'll probably give me what for for not stopping by."

Before he could mount up, the swinging doors to Dunlap's Saloon flew open. A wizened, bewhiskered man tore down the wooden sidewalk bellowing, "Somebody get the sheriff!"

Matt gave the old man a disgusted look when he stumbled across the street to where Matt stood beside his horse. The one blight on this town was the saloons that kept cropping up. He'd been glad when Captain Mace turned his saloon into a hotel a few years back, but another saloon just sprang up in its place—and another, and another, until there were more saloons than churches in Matt's beloved town.

"What's the trouble, Dan?" he asked the wheezing, wide-eyed man. "Can't Dunlap keep control of his customers?"

Dan Doyle reached out to steady himself against Matt's horse. "It's bad, Matt. Some wild-eyed, greenhorn kid came tearin' into the saloon yellin' that a two-legged skunk stole his horse. Like t'near started tearin' the place apart."

"Sounds like the usual scuffle. What's got you so fired up?"

Dan was breathing hard. " 'Cause he's just a kid, and it's Red Fallon he's accusin'."

Matt caught his breath. It sounded like this wasn't the usual fray that went on behind barroom doors. Red had a mean streak. He was an excellent cowhand, but the fiery redhead couldn't control his temper or hold his liquor—facts that kept him drifting from job to job. Against his better judgment Matt had hired Red on for the fall roundup. Now it already looked like he was going to regret it.

"I can't stay and jaw with you, Matt," Dan burst out. "I gotta get the sheriff quick, or there's gonna be a killin'. You oughta go over there and see if you can step in. Red's one of yer hands."

"I suppose you're right." Matt grimaced, set his jaw, and stepped into the street.

"Watch yourself, Matt." Dan gave a final warning. "Red's got a knife."

Matt grunted and hitched Chase to the rail again. A few long strides across the street and a mighty shove of the swinging doors put Matt inside the saloon—a place he only entered when he was obliged to round up some of his Diamond S hands after an occasional Saturday-night binge. The scene before him was one of wild confusion—just as Dan had described. Red Fallon towered over a stripling lad, knife in one hand, his other fist upraised. His steel gray eyes gleamed; a dangerous smile showed through his unkempt red beard.

The kid, who looked to be eighteen or nineteen, shook as he lay on the sawdust-covered floor. Matt sensed it was from rage, not fear. Blood poured from his nose. One eye was nearly swollen shut, and he was gasping for breath. His hand clutched his other arm, which told Matt that Red's knife had probably been busy. Clearly undaunted, the kid glowered at the hulking cowhand.

In spite of himself, Matt grinned. Although the kid was roughed up pretty bad, he didn't look beaten. Matt expected the boy to go after Red again at any moment. He could see it in the flashing blue eyes. *Down but not out. Thinks he can take on a grizzly bear! Just like Robbie.* In a flash the memory of Matt's little brother—much younger—going after Matt came to mind. His grin widened. A pair of cubs, neither of whom would admit defeat no matter what.

Matt was right. Uttering a shriek reminiscent of an Indian war cry, the youth sprang to his feet and lurched at Red, ramming his head into the big man's belly. With a surprised *oof*, Red reeled back, right into Matt's arms.

six

"What's going on in here?" Matt demanded of the cowhand. He heaved Red away from the boy, who was stumbling around, flailing his arms, and trying to stay on his feet.

"I'll kill that little upstart!" Red bellowed, lunging past Matt with murder in his eyes. His knife flashed.

Quick as lightning, Matt lashed out and grasped Red's knife hand. A twist, and the knife thudded to the floor. Matt picked it up, brushed away the sawdust, and laid it on the bar.

Red glared at Matt. "This ain't your affair, Boss." He pointed a meaty finger at the kid. "This is between me and him." He took a step toward the youth, who backed away, still clutching his arm. Blood flowed freely between his fingers, but he didn't seem to notice.

Matt stepped between them. "I'll ask you once more, Red, and I want a straight answer. What in blue blazes is going on?"

"That's what I'd like to know," a deep voice said from the saloon door. Sheriff Meade elbowed his way past the onlookers and glowered at the two men in the middle of the room.

"I'll tell you what's going on," the bloody but unbeaten lad shouted. He pointed an accusing finger at Red Fallon. "He stole my horse and supplies two days ago. I had to hoof it here without food and water." The lad's dusty shirt, jeans, and boots gave credence to his statement. He shook his fist at Red. "Copper's hitched outside this very minute!"

"That's a mighty serious accusation, son," Sheriff Meade quietly said. "Can you prove it?"

"Naw, he can't prove it!" Red bawled. His nostrils flared.

41

"I found that sorrel wandering around up near Raymond when I was going after strays the other—"

"Liar!" The boy leaped.

Matt caught him easily and steered him away from the enraged Red Fallon. "Take it easy, boy. No sense gettin' killed over a horse. Simmer down and let the sheriff get to the bottom of it." He looked into the kid's battered face, "What's your name?"

"Seth. Seth Anderson. And that ugly skunk is a lying horse thief." He made one more attempt to get at Red, then his eyes rolled back into his head, and he collapsed in Matt's arms.

Matt stared down at the unconscious youth. Seth's face was pale and gaunt beneath the dark bruises. Matt motioned to a couple of spectators. "Jake, you and Murray take this poor kid over to Mace's Hotel and ask Doc Brown to have a look at him. He's lost a lot of blood. I'll be along after a while." He gently placed Seth's limp body into the men's care and rounded on his erring cowhand. "There was no call to beat up that boy. Why'd you do it?"

"Boss, I don't take kindly to being accused of stealin' a man's horse and supplies. I tell you, I found that horse up in the foothills. There was nobody around." Red shrugged and spread his range-hardened hands. "Figured some feller met his end up near the mines. Why should I let a good piece of horseflesh wander off?"

"When you found out the horse belonged to Seth, why didn't you just give it back?" Matt wanted to know. He frowned. Something didn't ring true with Red's story, no matter how plausible it sounded. Or how aggrieved and innocent the cowboy acted.

"Why, Boss." Red grinned and reached for his knife. "That wildcat kid burst in here madder'n a hornet, demanding to know who owned the sorrel gelding tied up outside. 'Course

I told him it was mine." He examined his knife and slid it carefully into the sheath hanging from his belt. "He just lit into me after that."

"Yeah, Red. After you baited him," Charlie Dunlap piped up from behind the bar. He mimicked Red's voice. "Hey, fellers, any of you missin' a sorrel? No kid like this one's got a horse like that, 'nless he stole him. Know what we do to horse stealers 'round here?" Charlie scowled, "Sure young Anderson pitched into you. No self-respectin' feller, kid or not, would take that guff—and I notice you took almighty pleasure in beatin' the stuffin' out of him!"

A murmur of assent swept through the onlookers.

The sheriff's disbelieving snort showed his opinion of Red's story and confirmed Matt's suspicions. "Let's take a look at the horse."

With Sheriff Meade in the lead, Matt, Red, and a crowd of interested bystanders left the saloon and approached the sorrel Seth had referred to as "Copper." The tired animal stood with drooping head, showing he'd been ridden hard. But his ears perked up and he whinnied when the sheriff laid a gentle hand on his mane.

Matt whistled softly. "Nice horse. No wonder the kid was upset to find him missing or stolen."

Red glowered at his boss at the word *stolen* but kept his mouth shut. Sheriff Meade opened a saddlebag and pulled out a change of clothes. "These look like they might fit young Anderson." He sighed. "But without more evidence, I don't know how I can just hand this horse over to some stray kid who claims the sorrel's his."

"What about this?" Matt asked from the other side of the horse. He held up a wrinkled and faded photograph. "It might be a picture of his family. One of them is a good likeness of Seth. The others. . ." His voice trailed off as he gazed at the faces of two women. One was an older woman who clearly resembled Seth. The other—

Matt held his breath at the picture of the. . .girl? No. Not a girl but a young lady. She was seated next to the woman he decided must be their mother. Matt was struck by the girl's clear, steady gaze and the look of quiet honesty on her young face. A pretty face. Innocent with a look of fun and laughter waiting to be set free. Not beautiful, but Matt had no interest in beauty. *"Favour is deceitful, and beauty is vain. . . ."* He'd learned that the hard way from Lydia Hensley a few years back. Quickly he passed the photograph to Sheriff Meade.

The sheriff gave the photo a brief glance and announced his decision. "Appears to me this sorrel belongs to Seth Anderson." He caught Red's baleful gaze, held up a weather-beaten hand when Red started to speak, and said, "Don't get your back up, Red. I want to hear the boy's side of this before I make any final judgment. He ain't up to talking and probably won't be for a while. I'm gonna overlook the beating you gave the kid—for now. But if that boy's injuries prove serious, I'm taking you in. This is the third cutting scrape this month, and I've had enough. Ben Hoder's still in jail waitin' trial for carving up Joe Mova so bad he died. You'll be joining him if you're not careful."

Red's face turned livid. "You can't arrest me for—"

"That's what you think." Sheriff Meade strode off, his boot heels clumping heavily on the wooden sidewalk outside the saloon.

"Get back to the ranch," Matt barked, "before I decide I'd rather go shorthanded this season than put up with your shenanigans."

"Ain't got no horse," Red whined. "Sold him when I got the sorrel."

"A shame." Matt shook his head, not sorry in the least. "I

suggest you go buy him back. Then get out to the ranch." He raised a warning finger at the man. "And I don't want this incident brought up again, is that clear?"

A curt nod was all Matt got for a response. The big cowhand turned on his heel and took off down the street.

A sigh of relief whispered through the crowd. The interested bystanders went about their business. Matt made sure Seth would be all right then mounted Chase and headed back to the Diamond S—thanking God he had chosen to ride into town this morning. His thoughts kept time to the rhythmic beat of the buckskin's hooves on the parched ground. Who was Seth Anderson? Where had he come from? Judging by his ragged, dusty clothing, he'd been on the trail for some time.

Were the woman and girl in the picture really the young man's mother and sister? Matt laughed. "Why should I care, Chase?" The gelding flicked his ears but didn't change his stride. "I do though. He's a game kid, just like Robbie." A pang went through Matt. "God, I miss Robbie so much. I don't know why he had to die so young." He forced his thoughts back to the present. "I hope Seth will be all right. I'd hate for anything to happen to him. He must be a pretty good sort, with a mother and sister like that. Looks like he could use some help. If he pulls through, I'll see what I can do."

Long before Matt reached the Diamond S, he had spun dreams of bringing Seth Anderson to the ranch and teaching him the tricks of the range—the same way he had once taught Robbie. Matt smiled. "Lord, if I'm a good judge of character—and I am—this tenderfoot kid will take to life on the Diamond S like Chase to a water trough on a hot day. He's as spunky as Dori, and with her off at school, it will be good to have someone like him around the place again." Stirrings of anticipation brought a laugh. "Oh boy, when she comes home, those two will liven up the ranch like fireworks on the Fourth of July!"

ૐ

Eighteen months later, Matt knew it had to be the good Lord who'd literally dropped Seth Anderson into his lap that dusty fall afternoon. After hearing from Doc Brown that the lad's injuries were not life threatening but merely a temporary annoyance, Matt had offered to free Captain Mace from having to care for the young stray. The tourist season was in full swing, and the captain had plenty to oversee. His hotel was crowded with guests waiting to take the Yosemite Stage and Turnpike Company's ninety-mile trip up ten thousand feet to enjoy the awesome grandeur of Yosemite Valley. In addition, the captain and his crew provided a hearty supper for the southbound passengers of the Southern Pacific Railroad when it stopped in Madera each evening. It was too much to ask the generous hotel proprietor to care for a boy who would need vigilant attention over the next few weeks. The Diamond S was the perfect place for Seth to recuperate.

seven

No one understood why Matt wanted to take on the still-wet-behind-the-ears kid.

"It's roundup, Matt. Are you loco?" the captain protested when Matt showed up with his wagon to transport the young man out to his ranch. "You've got no time to mollycoddle a greenhorn, especially one who probably won't be leaving his bed for the next month."

Matt couldn't deny that even without the beating from Red, Seth didn't look much like a candidate for ranch work.

"More like a shopkeeper," his foreman, Brett Owen, joked when he saw him.

Matt didn't explain why he wanted Seth out at the Diamond S. Or that something about the lad called out for help—help he hadn't been able to give his younger brother. So Matt brought Seth home to the Diamond S and placed him under the gentle, ministering hands of his family's longtime housekeeper, Solita. At once the round-faced, cheerful Mexican woman clucked and fussed over Seth as if he were a long-lost chick returning to the nest. *Perhaps he is*, Matt mused on more than one occasion. The more he became acquainted with Seth Anderson, the more the young man reminded Matt of his younger brother, Robert.

Robbie had worshipped the ground Matt walked on. He had followed him everywhere. Five years Matt's junior, Robbie tried to do everything his older brother did. The boy's desire to keep up with Matt often led him into trouble. Occasionally he lit into Matt in frustration when he found himself lacking the skills necessary to do whatever his brother did. Matt prayed for patience, took it all in stride, and tried to be the big brother he should be.

Unfortunately Robbie tried to keep up once too often. Matt, at twenty, had excelled at the ranching tasks he loved. His father, William, depended on Matt to help run the growing Diamond S spread. Matt could rope, ride, and brand just about anything on four hooves. He could break a colt gently or all at once.

Fifteen-year-old Robbie wanted to prove he could do it, too. Although forbidden to work with the green colts, he took it upon himself to try to break Skye—the wildest colt on the ranch. Matt found his little brother one afternoon— broken and near death. He lived two more days before passing quietly from Matt's arms into heaven.

Now, six years later—with his entire family either back east or in eternity—Matt saw in Seth a replica of the brother who had been snatched away from him too soon. Every day he grew closer to the plucky boy.

Fall roundup ended, and Matt devoted all his spare time to working with his newest cowhand. Seth healed rapidly and seemed anxious to please his benefactor. Although weak and shaky at times, the young man made up for his inexperience with the determination to conquer every task Matt set for him. The older and more seasoned hands watched in amusement and shouted good-natured barbs at Seth while their boss tried to teach him basic ranching skills.

"Ride 'em, cowboy!"

"Straddle that saddle, kid!"

Seth ignored the banter and raw jokes and focused every ounce of his willpower into mastering the various jobs on the Diamond S. To the astonishment of the skeptical Diamond S cowboys, Seth learned quickly. Even trail-hardened Brett

Owen finally admitted—although not in Seth's hearing—"He's worth his salt." High praise indeed. It summed up the growing respect for Seth's hard work and stubborn determination.

By spring good food and steady exercise combined with the mild climate of Madera turned the stripling lad into a well-muscled and agile young cowboy. Once he proved himself adept at working with cattle and horses, haying, cutting fence posts, and the myriad of other duties a cowboy must do, Seth was welcomed into the ranks as a full-fledged cowhand, ready to pull his weight to make the Diamond S prosper. By summer he was one of the top hands.

During this time, Matt learned about his young friend's hardships back East. Often after church on Sunday afternoons, while the rest of the cowhands took the day off to head for town to court, cockfight, gamble, or take part in some other activity Matt preferred not to know about, he and Seth rode to Matt's favorite spot on the ranch—some distance into the Sierra foothills—and talked. The promontory that overlooked Matt's ranch offered both privacy and beauty. The entire valley spread out before them, dotted with dark clumps of the vineyards and orchards that were quickly springing up north of the San Joaquin River. Closer to their lookout, the rolling range was sprinkled with Diamond S cattle roaming freely.

A faint lowing sound drifted up to Matt's ears, and he sighed, perfectly content. "Must've been a hard thing to do, leaving your ma and sister back in St. Louis like that," he remarked, resting his long, lean body against the trunk of an old oak tree.

Seth lay down, settled his wide-brimmed hat over his eyes, and clasped his hands behind his neck. "Worse than you can imagine. But my mother knew I had no choice. She was hoping I could save enough money to bring Sarah out West someday." He peeked out from under his hat. "I showed you her picture, didn't I?"

Matt leaned forward and flopped his hands over his raised knees. He smiled patiently. "Often enough."

"Do you think she's pretty?"

"Oh, yeah. Sure, kid," came Matt's distracted reply. This was dangerous territory. He didn't want to hurt Seth's feelings, but he really wasn't interested in thinking about whether the girl in Seth's wrinkled photo was pretty or not. He glanced at his friend, who had sat up and was rummaging through his vest pockets.

"I know I've got another picture of her around here somewhere," Seth muttered. "It's more recent. I sent my folks a letter back in July."

"Hmm," Matt answered, not really paying attention. Watching Chase graze, he thought how dry and unappetizing the late October grass must taste—even to a horse.

"I sent a picture of the two of us," Seth prattled on, "you know, when that fancy Eastern photographer, who set up shop next to Judge Barry's office, was offering a special during the Fourth of July celebration. It turned out real fine, and I sent it to my mother and Sarah—so they'd see I'm doing okay."

Matt didn't answer, but Seth persisted. "I got a letter yesterday from Sarah—and she sent another photograph. You want to see it?"

Matt yawned. "The picture or the letter?"

Seth gave Matt a disgusted look and passed him the photograph.

Matt sat up and glanced at the picture. Against his will his eyes widened. His pulse quickened. This young woman couldn't be the same girl he'd seen in the photograph he'd dug out of Seth's saddlebags the year before! She was more than pretty—she was striking. Her clear gaze—no doubt the same color blue as Seth's—riveted Matt. She seemed to be smiling just for him.

Stop it! he berated himself. *It's not like you to get moonstruck over a picture!* He swallowed and quickly handed it back to Seth. "Real nice, kid," he managed. "I sure hope you can get her out here, like your ma wants. From what you've told me, your sister's life sounds pretty rotten." If Matt ever saw that low-down sidewinder of a stepfather, he'd have a thing or two to say to him about the way a man should treat his wife and children!

Seth sighed. "I don't know if Sarah will ever come out now." He held up a well-handled piece of paper. "This letter says that my mother is in the family way. Guess I'll be getting a new little brother or sister sometime next spring." He shrugged. "No matter. I'll probably never see the baby—or Sarah, for that matter." He stuffed the picture and letter into his vest pocket and stared out across the valley, quiet all of a sudden.

Matt straightened up, suddenly ashamed for treating the photograph of Seth's sister lightly. He'd "adopted" Seth so completely that he occasionally forgot the young man had a mother and a sister whom he must love dearly—just as Matt loved Dori. "Hey, Seth," he apologized gruffly, "I'm sorry. Real sorry about the hard times with your family. As soon as your mother is settled with the new little one, no doubt Sarah will be able to come out to the Golden State." He smiled and punched his young friend lightly on the shoulder.

Seth didn't smile. "Sarah wrote that Mama will need her more than ever once the baby comes. She's fixed her mind on staying." He looked at Matt. Misery showed on his tanned face. "My stepfather will work her to death, most likely, or marry her off to one of his disreputable acquaintances." Seth clenched his fists and drove them into the ground. "And I'm helpless. Helpless to do anything but watch it happen. I almost dread another letter."

❧

Seth received no more letters. The following spring a telegram came to Seth, in care of the Diamond S Ranch, Madera, California. His sister had been born. But his mother and the baby had died.

Matt's heart ached with pity and the pain of remembering his own losses. Now the boy who had carved out a special place in Matt's heart would need his friendship more than ever.

"He will have it," Matt vowed one afternoon while returning from town. "For as long as he wants to stay, the Diamond S will be Seth Anderson's home." Comfortably slumped in the saddle, Matt gave Chase free rein and let his thoughts drift like a tumbleweed skipping along with the slight breeze. Feelings that had been growing ever since the telegram came surfaced then burst into full-fledged determination. They spilled into a prayer that hovered in the quiet air.

"God, if there's any possible way to get Sarah Joy Anderson out of her stepfather's clutches, please show me what it is. For Seth's sake," he hastily added.

Only for Seth's sake? a little voice whispered inside him. Matt tried to ignore it, but the face in Seth's photograph shimmered in the quiet air until Matt whacked Chase with the reins. The unaccustomed blow, light as it was, sent the startled buckskin into a gallop guaranteed to banish the mirage and bring any once-bitten, twice-shy rancher back to his senses.

eight

Nineteen hundred miles east of the Diamond S Ranch, Sarah wearily rose from her corn-husk mattress at the crack of dawn. She shivered in the early morning chill and hastily wrapped herself in her mother's old dressing gown. The tattered garment not only offered warmth but also the feeling of being enfolded in her mother's arms, comfort that Sarah sorely needed. Ever since Gus had sold her to Tice Edwards—being sold was exactly what it amounted to—Sarah's days had been filled with continued drudgery and her nights with fear. Nights in which she racked her brain to think of a way to escape.

So far none had appeared, in spite of her desperate prayers for God to make a way. Now she sighed and reached for her mother's Bible. During the final weeks of Mama's illness, Sarah had let her scripture reading fall by the wayside from lack of time and energy. "Lord, I'm stuck in St. Louis until I can figure out how to earn enough money to leave here," she whispered into her harsh pillow, careful not to disturb her sleeping half sister. If Ellie awakened, all chances of quiet time for Sarah would flee before the petulant child's demands.

Sarah knelt on the rough floor beside the window and stared out into a day as gray as her life. "I need the wisdom of Solomon to know how to endure Tice's unwelcome advances, God. He's made his intentions clear—he will court me briefly and then wed me."

Fierce determination surged through Sarah's body. She would not marry Tice. She would kick and scream and tear the wedding gown he had ordered made for her until everyone in St. Louis heard. Surely someone would come to her rescue!

Who? a little voice mocked. *Tice Edwards has this town, including the police chief and who knows how many others, in the palm of his hand.* Despair threatened to overwhelm her, but words her father had spoken long ago swept into her heart. Sarah could picture his face, haggard from illness, when he said: *"Seth, Sarah, you will be faced with many hard decisions throughout your life. There is only one way to choose rightly. First, consider all the possibilities and the likely consequences. Next, take them to the Lord in prayer. Finally, wait for His answer."*

He had raised his head with a look so loving and kind Sarah knew she would never forget it. *"Most importantly, once you make your decision, go straight forward, not looking to the right or the left, and carry it out. If it later needs to be altered, our heavenly Father will guide you."*

He hesitated a long moment, closing his eyes as if he needed to gather strength. When he opened them again, a smile lifted his lips, and the blue eyes so like Seth's and Sarah's twinkled. *"Most folks disagree, but I believe it's better to make a decision that may later have to be amended than refuse to make any decision at all."*

That is what Seth did, Sarah thought. A spurt of courage raised her spirits, but again, that dreaded word *how* sent them plummeting. She shifted her position and opened the Bible, which had been her parents' answer book to all their problems. A letter fell out. A letter with the words *Sarah Joy* inscribed on the envelope in her mother's handwriting. With a quick glance to make sure the rustling paper hadn't awakened Ellie, Sarah opened the letter.

Dearest Daughter Sarah, it began. A rush of tears blinded her, but she impatiently brushed them away and read on:

*You may never see this letter. If everything goes well with
my birthing, I will burn it. However, I can't help feeling
that God may take me home—both me and your new little
brother or sister. There are things I must say to you in case
this happens.*

*First of all, I know you will grieve for me, but you must
also rejoice. My love for you and Seth has been my only
joy for a long time. You have been everything a son and
daughter should be. Your father and I chose our children's
names long before either of you were born. Sarah—princess;
Seth—anointed.*

*I did a terrible thing when I married Gus. I knew he could
never replace my beloved John, but he seemed sincere and
a good Christian. I truly believed his promise to become a
substitute father.*

Sarah stopped reading. Pity for her mother who had paid
so dearly for her error in judgment warred with anger at Gus.
Substitute father? Never! From the moment he said, "I do,"
Virginia Anderson Stoddard and her two children meant
nothing to him but persons he could exploit. Sarah shook off
the past. What was done was done. The important thing was
what lay ahead. She returned to her mother's precious letter:

*Sarah Joy, should it be that I cross over, I urge you to leave
St. Louis as quickly as you can and never look back. Find
Seth. Put yourself under his protection.*

"How?" Sarah murmured. "Long before I could earn any
money, Gus and Tice will have me married and trapped forever."
Ellie stirred in her sleep, sending a warning chill through
Sarah. She hastily read the final sentences of her mother's
letter:

Tucked away in the bottom of the flour barrel is a small tin canister. In it you will find enough money to get away from St. Louis. I scraped and pinched to set aside a few gold coins for you. The gold wedding ring your father gave me is also in the canister. If the need arises, sell it. You must get away from Gus. There is no telling what he might take a notion to do.

Your Loving Mother,
Virginia Anderson

Sarah wanted to shout. Her mother had been a faithful wife, but Gus Stoddard wasn't worthy of having his name on Mama's last message. Sarah kissed it then swiftly and silently donned her old blue calico work dress and hid the letter inside next to her heart. The words of the "Old Hundredth" came to mind, written centuries before:

Praise God, from Whom all blessings flow;
Praise Him, all creatures here below;
Praise Him above, ye heavenly host;
Praise Father, Son, and Holy Ghost.

She silently whispered "Amen" and crept downstairs, avoiding the timeworn, creaking boards. Step by cautious step, she stole to the kitchen. Once there she raised the lid of the flour barrel with trembling fingers—then froze when a familiar, hated voice demanded.

"What're you doin', sneakin' around?" Disheveled and glaring, Gus Stoddard stood in the doorway watching her like a hawk watches baby chicks before pouncing.

Please, God, help me! If Gus finds the money and Mama's ring, I'm doomed.

Summoning the courage generated by her mother's letter,

Sarah turned and said in a colorless voice, "Making biscuits. I woke up early." She reached into the barrel and filled the battered sifter with flour.

Some of the suspicion in Gus's face dwindled. An evil grin replaced it. "Sooooo," he drawled, "can't wait to see Tice, huh?"

Sarah shrugged, as if indifferent to the riverboat gambler and his intentions.

"I see you're gettin' used to the idea. Good. You make a fuss, and it will be the worse for you, missy," Gus warned.

Strength flowed into Sarah. She looked directly into Gus's face and managed to smile. "I won't make a fuss. I promise." Truth underlined every word, even though she mentally added, *I won't be here to make a fuss.* For the first time since Mama had fallen ill, happiness filled Sarah. No matter how long and hard the path ahead was, thanks to Virginia *Anderson*, her daughter would be free.

It was late afternoon before Sarah could retrieve the canister. Once emptied, it took its place on a kitchen shelf with nothing to indicate it had once contained treasure. Finished with her many chores for a few moments, Sarah opened her mother's Bible again. She riffled the pages and stopped at Matthew 10:16: "Behold, I send you forth as sheep in the midst of wolves: be ye therefore wise as serpents, and harmless as doves." It was underlined. Sarah resolved to take her mother's advice and secretly prepare to leave—all the while pretending to accept the inevitable future Gus and Tice had planned for her. Perhaps in that way she would throw them off guard.

Yet in spite of her determination, it was all Sarah could do to keep her fear and dislike of Tice Edwards from spilling out when he came courting. She had to admit that he never showed her anything but gentle, considerate attention. He took her for buggy rides and painted a glowing, wonderful picture of their future.

"You will love life on the *River Queen*," he assured her over and over. "Can't you just imagine gliding down the river and watching glorious sunrises and sunsets?"

Sarah nodded. She could imagine it all right—with horror, not anticipation.

Tice never let her forget him for more than a short time. He wrote flowery letters when he couldn't come in person. He brought her nosegays, not wildflowers but expensive bouquets from the best flower sellers in St. Louis. He arranged for the best dressmaker in St. Louis to fashion Sarah's wedding gown. Raging inside, she passively stood while the woman measured, cut, and draped. She must not arouse suspicion, even though she would rather wear faded calico all her life than spend one minute in the expensive gown Tice had selected.

He also bought her costly little trinkets. Sarah shrank from accepting anything from her would-be husband but privately gritted her teeth and stashed them away for her journey. Anything small enough to carry that she could sell would help. Between visits, Sarah continued her hard, monotonous tending of the house and trying to manage the children. In spare moments she started gathering the supplies she would need for her trip to California.

Sarah occasionally felt overwhelmed at the enormity of what she was attempting.

Nineteen hundred miles lay between St. Louis and the Diamond S Ranch near Madera, California. Nineteen hundred mind-staggering miles filled with unknown dangers. At those times Sarah took comfort in rereading Seth's letters, which soon became ragged. Countless times she looked at the photograph he'd sent and imagined life in the West. Against her better judgment her imagining always included the dark-haired stranger with Seth. Her brother surely couldn't be wrong about Matthew Sterling's character. If only Tice were the man the young rancher appeared to be!

She laughed bitterly. Despite his suave sophistication, Tice Edwards was no better than Gus Stoddard. Marrying him would be like the old saying, "Leaping out of the frying pan into the fire."

"Never," Sarah vowed again and again, thanking God for her mother's far-reaching wisdom and attention to her daughter's need to escape when she was gone.

During one of the times of fanciful musing and the inevitable comparison between Matt Sterling and Tice Edwards, the children swarmed up the stairs, screaming for Sarah's attention. A few of Seth's letters and the photograph scattered to the floor. Sarah hastily gathered them up and shoved them into her reticule.

&

Sarah's precarious tightrope walk between appearing submissive and secretly plotting her escape ended long before she felt ready to steal away.

Her plans shattered one morning when Gus shuffled into the kitchen. His wide grin and triumphant expression set Sarah's nerves jangling. Tice was right behind Gus, wearing a look of satisfaction that chilled Sarah to the marrow.

"By tomorrow night you won't be doin' this, missy," Gus announced with a smirk. "Tice here says he's waited long enough and done enough courting. You'll be married tomorrow afternoon. Right, Tice?"

"Yes." Twin devils danced in the gambler's wicked black eyes. "I've been pining away for you long enough, Sarah."

She dropped a frying pan. It splashed soapy water on her apron and the floor, giving her time to hold her tongue instead of screaming and rushing out the open door. She started cleaning up the mess, desperately searching for words. Psalm 50:15 came to sustain her, as other familiar verses had done in the past few weeks: *"Call upon me in the day of trouble: I will deliver thee, and thou shalt glorify me."*

"Tomorrow? I hardly think that is possible," she began.

"It's your own fault," Gus growled. "Tice says you won't even let him kiss you until you're married."

It took every ounce of self-control to keep from shuddering. Kiss Tice Edwards? She'd sooner kiss a copperhead!

The two men took her silence for consent and strode out, slapping each other on the back and jesting in a crude way.

But Sarah bit her lip until it bled. Ready or not, she must slip away that night.

nine

From the time he was old enough to straddle a pony, Matthew Sterling's favorite season on the Diamond S had always been spring. For a short time a green carpet covered the brown and barren hills. The mud and rain took a break. New calves and foals and baby chicks appeared almost overnight. How Matt loved to see the colts and fillies kick up their heels in the pasture then flee to their mamas when startled.

Spring also had sounds of its own: the peeping of baby chicks, music to a child's ears. The clang of the triangle outside the cookshack and the stentorian command "Come and git it before I throw it out" that roused grumbling hands from their beds earlier than they had grown accustomed to rise during the slower winter months.

Whenever young Matt could escape his parents' watchful eyes, he delighted in sneaking out in his nightshirt to eat breakfast with the cowboys. He later laughed at the childhood glee he had felt at outwitting his parents. He hadn't found out until he was ten years old that he hadn't put anything over on them. William and Rebecca Sterling had recognized their son's need for independence even at that early age. Besides, no harm would come to Matt in either the cookshack or the bunkhouse. The hands adored the plucky little boy who manfully tried to ride everything that moved, including uncooperative cows, squealing pigs, and even a turkey whose tail came off in Matt's futile grab to keep from sliding off. If a laughing, hip-slapping cowboy hadn't rescued the youngster, Matt would have been in danger of being seriously pecked by the irate, partially denuded fowl. With Matt's penchant for mischief, it wasn't the last time a ranch hand came to his rescue.

The Sterlings' carefree life ended with the death of Matt's mother when he was only fifteen. Yet God had not forgotten the family, which had grown to include Robert and Dolores. In the midst of their sorrow, God sent Solita, whose name meant *little sun*. The round-faced Mexican housekeeper and cook more than lived up to her name. She not only brought sunlight back into the grieving family's dark world, but she also became a substitute mother. She spoiled the children rotten, especially "Matelito." But when Matt took his position as head of the family after his father's death, he became Senor Mateo to Solita, and she became his confidante and guiding light. Matt loved her dearly and was never too proud to seek and heed her advice.

The second spring after Seth Anderson came to the Diamond S meant that Matt, Seth, and the rest of the hands spent every waking moment outdoors as the ranch swung into full operation. This particular year, the amount of work was heavier than ever. A deep frown creased foreman Brett Owen's leathery face when he approached Matt and Seth, who were leaning on the corral fence, watching a frisky colt.

"This spring is fixin' to be the driest in years," Brett predicted. "How about drivin' the herd up to the high country early this year?"

"Good idea," Matt agreed. "The grazing down here is already getting mighty poor."

"Yippee-ki-ay. Up to the high country!" Seth leaped into the air, clicked his heels together, then reddened and looked sheepish. "Sorry, Boss. Sometimes I forget I'm not still a kid."

Brett shook his finger at Seth. "You ain't so all-fired old," he admonished. "And you'll live to be a lot older if you don't tangle with rustlers or all the other confounded trouble a feller meets while herdin' ornery cows." He turned on his heel and stomped off, but a loud *haw haw* floated back to the corral.

"He's right," Matt said quietly. "A man mean enough to steal another man's stock is either a coward or crazy. Either can be dangerous in the right circumstances." He lightly punched Seth's shoulder. "Let's go tell Solita we're going on a roundup." He grinned, knowing it was all Seth could do to restrain himself from yippee-ki-yaying again. For the hundredth—no, the thousandth—time, Matt thanked God for sending the young man so like Robbie to fill the empty spot in his life. Seth was totally absorbed in what he considered the best profession on earth: ranching. He was also loyal and true, a boy after Matt's own heart.

Seth had only one fault: the desire to draw Matt into the social doings of Madera. Although Matt enjoyed socializing with the townsfolk, he drew the line at getting involved with the fairer sex. He steadfastly declined Seth's invitations to any entertainment that would force him into their presence and compromise his stance.

"Why?" Seth wanted to know.

One day, Matt, in a fit of exasperation, blurted out, "When I was about your age, I met a girl I thought was an angel straight from heaven. She wasn't."

"Oh?" Seth cocked an eyebrow, obviously waiting for Matt to continue.

He didn't. Instead he walked off, feeling Seth's gaze bore into his back. But those few words opened a floodgate of memories that began five years earlier, memories Matt had thought were banished forever. . . .

Lydia Hensley was the daughter of the supervisor for the California Lumber Company from Chicago, sent out west to prepare for laying out the new town of Madera and the sale of the lots. Lydia was lonely, so far from home, so Matt received permission from her father to escort her to social engagements in Fresno—twenty-two miles south.

Lydia hit the San Joaquin Valley like a tornado. She created havoc among the young men and heartburn among the girls. Matt fell head over heels for the young miss the first time he saw her—a vision in a soft pink gown, white skin shaded by a ruffled pink parasol. She was the prettiest and brightest girl Matt had ever met. Time after time he wondered why he had been so fortunate to be chosen as her escort from the dozens of swains who flocked to her doorstep. Lydia's green eyes flashed with mischief or softened into languishing glances, depending on her mood. Not a single ash-blond hair ever seemed to be out of place.

The smitten Matt escorted Lydia to parties and dances all spring and summer. He sat by her in church. He took her on picnics, little realizing he'd been chosen to be the favored one not only for his good looks but because he owned the Diamond S and was considered a catch.

Lydia led Matt on, driving him to distraction. He lost interest in the ranch, left its running in Brett Owens's capable hands, and spent most of the season calling on Miss Lydia. He dreamed of making her queen of the Diamond S.

Love's young dream ended six months later when the surveying ended. Hensley and his daughter packed up to head back to civilization. Lydia's parting with Matt was a disaster. He managed to extricate her from the young people who had gathered for a farewell party and led her to a secluded alcove.

Heart beating double-time, Matt went straight to the point. "I can't let you go, Lydia. Will you marry me?" He held out a diamond ring the size and brilliance of which was unknown in the valley.

Lydia stared at the beautiful ring as if unwilling to let such a treasure slip through her white fingers. She stroked his lean face with a well-manicured hand and looked deep into his eyes, the sign of affection she often employed. An incredulous smile crossed her face. "Matthew Sterling, you don't really expect me to stay out here? I belong in Chicago where it is civilized. I do appreciate your asking me though." She glanced down then back up with the appealing look that brought suitors to their knees and subject to her will. "If you want me to take the ring to remember my Westerner, I'll be happy to do so."

Disillusionment swept through Matt like the San Joaquin River in flood. "Your Westerner, Lydia? Have you only been amusing yourself to pass the time?"

She had the grace to redden but tossed her head. "It was fun while it lasted. You'll have to admit that." She gave him the smile that had formerly bewitched him and now left him as cold and hard as the diamond in the ring he had so carefully selected. "About the ring—"

Scales fell from Matt's love-blinded eyes. He saw Lydia for what she was: a selfish, greedy girl out for all she could get. Brokenhearted he raised his head in a gesture that would have impressed anyone with the sensitivities of a turnip. Then he slipped the ring into his pocket and said, "You will have no keepsake to remember me by, Lydia." He marched out, head still high, like a one-man army with flags waving. And he vowed the San Joaquin River would run dry before he ever again trusted any girl or woman except Solita.

Matt had faithfully kept that vow until the wrinkled and much-handled picture of Sarah Anderson, taken just before her brother left home, kindled a spark of interest and admiration. Such an honest and steady gaze in the young girl's face. The delicate way her hands were clasped. Her eyes radiating love for her Seth and her mother. And all that beautiful hair, long and rippling to her waist.

The second picture threatened to undo the weeks, months, and years Matt had spent locking up his heart and throwing away the key. It didn't help when Seth asked Matt to take the picture as a favor.

"Maybe you could look at it occasionally and say a prayer for her and my mother. I worry about her constantly."

"I will, but I don't need the picture," Matt protested. Yet when Seth insisted, Matt's hands turned sweaty, and his heart beat unnaturally fast. He slipped the picture into the pocket inside his vest "as a favor to Seth," he reminded himself, and was never without it.

The image of Sarah's honest face rode sidesaddle with Matt across the California range even when he wasn't looking at it. In spite of his unwillingness to admit the rusty hinges of his heart were creaking open, the image of Sarah's sweet face was like oil to a long-unused lock. Over and over, Matt wondered how any man could treat an innocent girl the way Gus Stoddard treated Sarah. He found himself wishing he could intervene, "for Seth's sake, of course," he reminded himself.

Just before spring roundup, the town of Madera planned a money-raising event. Seth Anderson was wild to go. Matt was sitting in the kitchen watching Solita toss tortillas when Seth raced in. "What time are we leaving?"

Matt gave him a puzzled look. "Leaving for where?"

"To Madera. This Saturday. There's gonna be a baseball game and stuff for the little kids and a box social. I've never been to one. Gus didn't cotton to such, so even though he took us to church, we didn't get in on the fun. I've been saving my money to bring Sarah out West, but Solita can pack me a lunch. It will be fun to watch you bid on a young lady's box."

"Me!" Matt's stool tipped and threatened to spill him on the floor. "A box social is the last place I intend to go."

"You gotta go, Boss. It's to raise money to repair the church roof."

Matt stood. "I'll make a contribution."

Seth looked so disappointed that Matt relented. "Tell you what. I'll go to the game, and I'll give you some money to bid."

"It won't be half as much fun without you."

Seth's disappointed response convinced Matt. "Well, if it means that much to you, I suppose I could go and watch. But don't expect me to bid, no matter how fancified the boxes are or how much they smell of fried chicken and chocolate cake."

"Is that what they put in them?" Seth licked his lips. He staggered out holding his stomach, leaving Matt wondering why he'd agreed to appear at the social.

Solita told him, "It is good that you are going, Senor Mateo. There are many nice senoritas in Madera who will be glad."

"I am not going to make senoritas glad," Matt mumbled. "Did you cook this up with Seth?"

Solita placed her hands on her apron-covered hips. "Would I do such a thing?" she demanded, but Matt noticed she didn't deny his charge.

For the rest of the week, Matt felt like a trapped bobcat. On Saturday he reluctantly donned his best plaid shirt, tied on a red neckerchief, and crammed his Stetson down to his ears, feeling like he was headed to a hanging. By the time he and Seth reached Madera, the boy had lost some of his high spirits. With a pang of regret for being surly, Matt suggested they volunteer for the ball team.

Seth immediately perked up and showed a surprising amount of skill.

The dreaded box social finally began. Matt had never seen

such an array of ribbons, ruffles, and flowers as adorned the boxes, but he kicked himself for coming.

Evan Moore, Madera's portly postmaster, made a fine auctioneer. "Who'll start the bidding?" he called, holding up a box and sniffing it. "Smells like fresh-baked apple pie."

"Two bits."

"Two bits?" Evan looked outraged. "Twenty-five measly cents for this lovely basket? What kind of miser bids two bits?"

The crowd roared.

The bidder quickly raised his hand. "Sorry, I meant to offer six bits."

"Not good enough. This is worth at least a couple of good ol' American dollars. Dig deep, folks. None of us want to be dripped on next winter 'cause the church roof leaks."

One by one, the baskets sold. Seth bid twice but dropped out when others "dug deep." Only a worn shoe box tied with string remained. Evan held it up. "Almost through folks. What am I bid?"

Stone-cold, dead silence greeted his plea.

Evan cast an imploring glance toward Matt. Despite his resolve to have no part in the social, Matt's heart ached for the owner of the unattractive box. He opened his mouth.

Seth beat him to it. "I bid a half eagle." He fished a five-dollar gold piece out of his pocket and held it up. "It better be enough. It's all I've got."

The crowd gasped. Only one or two of the fancy boxes had sold for that much.

"Sold!" Evan shouted. "What lucky lady gets to eat supper with Seth Anderson?"

"Me. Bertha Bascomb." A wispy, white-haired old lady hobbled forward.

Seth led Bertha to a nearby table. When he opened the

box, a sour smell rushed out.

Matt's heart sank. Not only were the bread and cheese ancient, but Bertha was proudly lifting out the sorriest excuse for cake Matt had ever seen. If it hadn't been so pathetic, it would have been hilarious. Matt quickly said, "Mrs. Bascomb, I missed out on a box. Is there enough for three?"

"If you ain't too big an eater," she grudged. "I don't want to skimp on this young man."

Seth remained gallant. "My boss and I had a big dinner so there should be enough."

The two men somehow choked down the terrible meal, amid grinning townsfolk and cowboys. Looks of respect showed that Seth Anderson's kindly bid had endeared him to Madera.

❧

Matt's stomach had barely recovered from the box social when a few days later a young lad galloped up to the Diamond S corral where Matt and Seth were leaning against the fence. He reined in his horse and leaped from the saddle.

Matt blinked in surprise. "What are you doing here, Johnny? And how come you're in such an all-fired hurry?"

Johnny rubbed a grimy hand over his freckled, sweaty face. "Telegram. Mr. Moore said I was s'posed to get it here pronto."

Matt's heart lurched. A lump as solid as Bertha Bascomb's sour bread and heavy cake formed in the pit of his stomach. He hated telegrams, especially since Dori had gone back east. Had something happened to her? Matt shook his head. It was far more likely that his impetuous sister had been expelled from the eastern academy she attended. Matt had received previous warnings about Dori's conduct. Her shortcomings had only been tolerated by the grace of God and several generous contributions to the prestigious Brookside Finishing

School for Young Ladies in Boston.

Matt reached for the telegram.

Johnny shook his head. "It ain't for you, Matt," he said. "It's for Seth." He tossed a soiled envelope to the younger man. "From St. Louis."

Seth's face went paper white.

Alarm shot through Matt as Seth ripped open the message. "Is it about Sarah?" he demanded. "Bad news?"

Seth looked stricken. *"The worst."*

"Well?" Matt's question cracked like a bullwhip.

"Read it for yourself." Seth thrust the telegram at Matt, eyes filled with pain and hopelessness.

Matt snatched the message and read:

SARAH DISAPPEARED *STOP* MAY COME TO MADERA *STOP* HOLD FOR FIANCÉ TICE EDWARDS AND ME *STOP* GUS STODDARD

The words slashed at Matt's heart like a hunting knife, cutting and tearing until he could barely breathe. Sarah engaged to be married? "Who is this Tice Edwards fellow?" he demanded.

Seth looked defeated. "A real rat. Everyone in St. Louis knows him. He owns a riverboat where folks go to gamble."

Matt caught his breath. Such a monstrous thing couldn't be true. Not when he had fallen in love with her picture. How could such a sweet and innocent-looking girl be promised to a riverboat gambler?

ten

The news that Tice planned to wed her the following day sent Sarah into a panic. She must disappear. Tonight. But how? At least Gus and Tice hadn't waited until evening to spring the bad news. By midnight the children would be asleep, and the two men she hated and feared most would probably be having an early celebration: Tice, knowing tomorrow he would have her in his control, and Gus, ecstatic at having his six-thousand-dollar debt forgiven and at receiving unlimited gambling privileges.

Sarah checked the time. It wasn't quite six. No wonder Gus had been grumpy. After his nights of gambling and carousing, he tended to sleep much later. "Lord," she whispered while beating the biscuit dough until it threatened to fight back, "I have eighteen hours. If I fly around and finish my chores quicker than usual, I should be able to make it."

A single glance around the shack sent hope plummeting to her toes. The place had never looked worse. How could she accomplish everything from washing the streaked windows to scrubbing the worn floor? She also needed to bake and wash clothes. Gus would rage if, on what he considered a special day, things weren't spick-and-span. Sarah set her jaw in a manner that boded no good. If she did all that needed doing, she wouldn't have a smidgen of time for herself. She would not bake bread. She would not wash clothes. They could wait until tomorrow—and by then she'd be gone. Fleeting pity for the burden soon to fall on Ellie's eight-year-old shoulders stirred Sarah, but she shrugged it off. Let Tice hire someone to help. Or as Gus had said, he could always get a woman to replace his long-suffering wife.

Sarah patted out her biscuits with well-floured hands, planning as she worked. *If I can catch Timmy alone and offer him a cookie he might help me,* she decided. *There's no use asking the boys or Ellie for help, even if they were around. They'd make a worse mess just to be ornery.* Her fingers itched to get started sweeping and cleaning instead of cooking mush and setting out butter and jam. Thank goodness they were out of bacon and eggs. Gus would roar, but when she'd asked for money to replenish the larder, he'd refused to give her any.

The ticking clock counted off the racing minutes until seven of Sarah's precious hours had been swallowed up in hard work. Sarah grew so frustrated she wanted to stomp her feet and throw a tantrum like Ellie did when she didn't get her own way. Hindrance after hindrance continued to rise, as if conspiring against her. Instead of staying away with his cronies as usual, Gus popped in and out of the house, commenting on how well Sarah was doing for herself by marrying Tice. She longed to hurl bitter words at him but bit her tongue and reminded herself that, by this time tomorrow, she'd be shut of him.

Not so for Ellie and Timmy. The older boys could fend for themselves, but the younger children would be at Gus's mercy. Sarah was almost glad when the youngsters acted up worse than ever before, fighting and demanding her attention. The last straw was when Sarah forcibly separated them and ordered them outside.

Ellie shrilled, "You ain't our ma. I hate you, and I'm glad you're going away. We don't have to do what you say. We're gonna get a new ma. Pa said so."

"And she ain't never, ever gonna tell us what to do," Timmy piped up, his face contorted with rage. He was so unlike the little boy who crept to Sarah for comfort it eased her guilt over leaving them, even though she could not stay.

"I feel like Job's granddaughter," she muttered to herself. "The way I've been plagued, the devil himself must be in league with Tice and this family today." She washed her hands and hot face, smoothed her hair, glanced around the cottage, and sighed. The place looked as good as she could make it, considering its shabby condition. Pale sunlight poured through the freshly washed windowpanes. Sarah had even washed the bedraggled calico curtains, and the floor smelled of the strong lye soap she'd used to scrub it to within an inch of its life. She'd relocated stacks of old newspapers and soiled clothing dropped at will by simply tossing them out of sight.

Reheated leftover stew and more biscuits had made up dinner an hour before. Sarah racked her brain to think of something for supper. Baked potatoes, maybe, and there was enough buttermilk. She'd make corn bread, open one of the last jars of fruit she had canned last fall, and serve the few cookies she had hidden from the children. Gus would complain, but she didn't care. It would be the last time she'd have to hear him rant and rave.

The clock struck one. It was time for her to go for the final fitting of her wedding dress.

Sarah sighed again. In spite of rushing, she wasn't one inch closer to being ready to steal out in the dead of night than she had been seven hours earlier. Now she had to spend precious time in a final fitting of the elaborate wedding gown Tice had selected for her. Sarah hated every inch of fancy lace, every tuck, every thread of the fine satin dress. She hated the cloud of a veil held by orange blossoms that would shroud her until her husband-to-be lifted it. Most of all she hated the imagined stares of those who came to gawk at her in her bridal white, the knowing glances exchanged between men as vile as Tice himself.

❧

By supreme self-control Sarah refrained from tearing the

wedding garments from her body and throwing them in the dressmaker's smug face when the woman purred, "What a beautiful bride you will be, *ma cherie*" in an accent as artificial as her smile. Sarah turned away. She had avoided looking at her mirrored image, but curiosity got the better of her. How would she look in bridal white should God someday send a man to love, honor, and cherish her? Not married wearing this lavish, pearl-beaded gown but in a modest white dress that did not silently shout its cost.

Sarah faced the full-length mirror. Her mouth fell open. Costly the gown might be but how it flattered her strawberry-blond hair, shining blue eyes, and the color in her blazing cheeks! A small smile trembled on her lips, adding the one factor needed to make the vision perfect. If only Matthew Sterling could see her in this gown!

Sarah closed her eyes and allowed herself the luxury of a dream. What would it be like to walk up the aisle of a church in Madera in step with her brother? To see dark-haired Matthew Sterling, tall, strong, and straight, waiting for her? To watch love and wonder spring into his eyes when he first caught sight of her—the same love and wonder that filled her heart and overflowed into the joyous occasion? To hear the time-honored words, "Dearly beloved, we are gathered here today to unite this man and this woman in holy matrimony. Marriage is ordained of God. . . ."?

Not this marriage!

Had she spoken aloud? No. The dressmaker was busily straightening a fold of the ostentatious train of the gown.

Sarah shuddered, but the picture of what a wedding could and should be had started a train of thoughts that could not be derailed. How she would welcome the opportunity to love and cherish a man such as Matt Sterling! Like Ruth in the Bible, she would unhesitatingly say, *"Intreat me not to leave thee, or to return from following after thee: for whither thou goest, I will go; and where thou lodgest, I will lodge: thy people shall be my people, and thy God my God."* Unlike marriage with Tice, she would not be unequally yoked. What she'd learned about Matt from Seth's secret letters had convinced her that Matt Sterling was a true Christian.

Her thoughts trooped on, repeating the majestic promises in the wedding service:

"For better. For worse. For richer. For poorer. In sickness. In health. Mutually agreeing to be companions. Forsaking all others. Keeping themselves for each other as long as they both should live." And finally *"Whom God hath joined together, let no man put asunder."* How did anyone dare take those vows lightly, only to break them as Gus had done. . .and as Sarah knew in her heart Tice would do?

"Does mademoiselle wish me to remove the gown?"

The dressmaker's question jerked Sarah from her wool-gathering. Her dream crumpled. It was highly unlikely that Matthew Sterling or someone like him would ever see Sarah Joy Anderson in a wedding dress. Worse, if her escape plan failed, only her miserable stepfamily, Tice Edwards, and his cohorts would gloat over the vision she had seen in the mirror. Depression filled her. Was this how maidens of old felt when forced into loveless marriages by domineering fathers desirous of forming strong alliances? Sarah's heart ached for all those denied the chance for true love and sacrificed on the altars of greed.

"Please take the dress off," she quietly said, ignoring the woman's babble and wishing only to slip into her own clothing.

When Sarah reached home, another two hours had passed. Now only nine of the eighteen remained. The relentless *tick tock, tick tock* of the clock greedily nibbled away at the day. It reminded Sarah of the "Grandfather's Clock" song that had come out a few years earlier. The chorus rang in Sarah's head:

Ninety years without slumbering, tick tock, tick tock,
His life seconds numbering, tick tock, tick tock,
It stopp'd short, never to go again, when the old man died.

"I won't be ninety, and my body won't die if I have to marry Tice Edwards, but my life will stop short," Sarah grimly told herself. "I feel like my seconds are being numbered, just like the grandfather's were."

Matthew 6:34 popped into her mind: *"Take therefore no thought for the morrow: for the morrow shall take thought for the things of itself. Sufficient unto the day is the evil thereof."*

In spite of her troubled heart Sarah couldn't help smiling. Today's evil was more than sufficient! The scripture cheered her up, and she resumed her duties with a lightened heart—until someone knocked on the door. Now what?

The "what" proved to be two fashionably dressed, strange women.

"Miss Anderson, we just *had* to come and call," one gushed.

"Yes," said the other. "Dear Mr. Edwards said you might appreciate our help, since you lost your dear mother so recently. So sad, just before your wedding." Her laugh grated like broken glass.

"Mama isn't lost," Sarah quietly said. "She's gone to heaven." She swallowed the words: *and there would be no wedding if she were here.*

The women gasped as if Sarah had shown bad taste in speaking so. "Oh, yes, of course," the gusher said. "Now what can we do? Last-minute arrangements and all that."

Sarah laughed. What would they think if they knew her "last-minute arrangements" consisted of packing what she could carry and fleeing from "dear Mr. Edwards" like a rabbit from a hound? "You're too kind." *As in kind of nosy.* "Thank you for coming, but things are in control." *In control of my heavenly Father.* "Now if you will excuse me. . ."

"Oh, to be sure. Come, Estelle." Clearly disappointed, the gusher took her friend's arm and sailed across the unkempt yard with a disapproving sniff that showed what she thought of "dear Mr. Edwards's" choice of a wife.

Sarah closed the door, leaned against it, and laughed until tears flowed. Taking advantage of an empty house, she raced to the attic. Gus and the children, perhaps even Tice, might appear at any time. She didn't know where they were, and she didn't care whether they were in school or playing hooky. Either way, one more day wouldn't make a difference.

She hastily gathered her things. The need to leave Seth's "treasures" behind saddened her. Sarah discarded most of her own as well—but not all. She took the tattered copy of *Little Women* Seth had found on the docks and her mother's worn dressing gown. The little wooden pistol Seth loved went into her reticule. She and her brother would at least have those reminders of their once-happy home.

Sarah feared the money her mother had hoarded for her wouldn't be enough for a quick trip west by rail. It seemed unwise to plunk down all she had in the world. She must count her pennies carefully, even if it took weeks or months to reach California. Perhaps she could find work along the way. She was pretty sure her stepfather would have no idea where she was headed. Sarah and her mother had taken great pains to keep Seth's location a secret.

When the clock struck midnight, Sarah slipped from her cot, praying the rustle of straw wouldn't awaken Ellie or the boys. The plan of escape hinged on Sarah's being able to sneak out undetected. With a silent prayer she began her long journey to freedom.

eleven

Sarah crept down the ladder from the loft and into the brooding St. Louis night, thankful when it closed around her and muffled her light footsteps. She started down the road toward Jefferson City, clutching her heavy carpetbag in one hand, her reticule in the other.

It was the longest night of Sarah's life, a night that taught her the true meaning of 1 Thessalonians 5:17: "Pray without ceasing." She jumped at the slightest sound. Passing hoofbeats drove her into hiding every few hours. "Lord, I know this is what You want me to do," she whispered. "I know You will be with me. But I'm still frightened. It is so far to California. Please help me be strong and not afraid."

The rising wind whisked away Sarah's prayer and fluttered the long cloak she had donned over her mother's worn, but still serviceable, Sunday-go-to-meeting dress. Sarah shivered and pulled the cloak closer, thankful both it and the dress were dark blue. With dark gloves, Virginia Anderson's old black hat pulled low, and a thick dark veil hiding her face, Sarah was next to invisible. Why, then, did concern over what Gus would do if he realized she had escaped haunt her? Every shifting shadow, every night noise set her heart pounding until it felt like it would burst.

A horrible screech from a nearby tree sent Sarah into a panic. She began to run, thankful for the few stars that broke through the murk to light her way. The unseen culprit screeched again. This time the flapping of wings followed.

Sarah stopped short. "You noisy bird," she told the owl that glided over her head. "Go on with your hunting. I'm too big to be your prey." She laughed softly. "Sarah Joy Anderson, if a stupid bird can scare you, how will you ever survive in California? There will be a lot more terrifying things there than a silly old hooting owl."

Not as terrifying as staying in St. Louis.

The thought dried up Sarah's laughter like drought parched a prairie. Nothing the unknown West might have in store for her could be more threatening than the horror of having to marry Tice Edwards.

Step-by-step, Sarah's shabby shoes carried her away from the gambler and her stepfather. In an effort to stem the nightmare image they conjured up, she began repeating scripture. A wave of gratitude filled her once more, as it had done all through her ordeal. Gratitude that John and Virginia Anderson had instilled in their children a love for the Bible and its promises from the time Seth and Sarah were born. Each verse from the psalms that Sarah murmured in the semidarkness quieted her troubled spirit. She ended by reciting: " 'In my distress I called upon the Lord, and cried unto my God: he heard my voice out of his temple, and my cry came before him, even into his ears.' "

When no more verses came to mind, Sarah fought the darkness surrounding her by softly singing hymns. Each brought comfort, most of all the hymn her mother had always sung when things with Gus became unbearable. Now, although Sarah kept her voice so low it didn't even carry to the treetops, the much-loved words came straight from her heart:

"He leadeth me! O blessed tho't!
O words with heav'nly comfort fraught!
What-e're I do, wher-e're I be,

Still 'tis God's hand that leadeth me.
"Sometimes 'mid scenes of deepest gloom,
Sometimes where Eden's bowers bloom—"

Sarah's voice broke. A river of tears crowded behind her eyes. Eden itself could be no more wonderful than reaching California and Seth. Her heart swelled, and she bowed her head. "There's a long, hard road ahead of me before I get to Madera. Please go before me and open the way." She took a deep breath. "I want to trust You, no matter what happens."

No peal of thunder answered Sarah's prayer. No bolt of lightning illuminated the road. But a still, small voice whispered deep inside, *"I will not only walk before you, Sarah Joy. I will walk beside you: your Savior, companion, and friend."*

Tears gushed. "Thank You, God," she fervently said. "I needed to be reminded like Elijah in the Bible. Your presence wasn't in the strong wind or the great earthquake but in the still, small voice." The still, small voice that spoke to Sarah's heart did what nothing else could accomplish. It increased her determination to throw herself totally on God's mercy and let Him take charge. Each step took her farther from Gus and Tice. Each hour meant that much more time before they raised a hue and cry over her absence.

By morning Sarah had traveled a goodly piece. However, lack of sleep had begun to take its toll. She ate sparingly from her small supply of food and drank from a nearby spring. A little later a farmer in a mule-driven wagon stopped beside her.

"Need a ride, miss?" he called.

Sarah looked into the farmer's kindly face. The steadiness of his faded blue eyes and the creases many years of living had etched in his trustworthy face reassured her.

"Yes, thank you." She climbed into the back of his wagon. She felt badly about not removing her veil but decided to leave it on. She *must not* be recognized in case Gus or Tice ever crossed paths with the old man. Surely they were searching for her by now, determined to make her go through with the wedding! Still, how could they know where she was? She had confided in no one and left no trace of her destination. Thankful that, although the farmer looked curious, he asked no questions about why she was alone on the road at such an early hour, Sarah gratefully dozed off and didn't rouse until he said, "Wake up, miss. This is where I turn off the main road." He pointed. "My farm's a mile or so down the lane."

He paused and looked worried. "Wish I could take you farther, but lots o' folks travel this way. You're sure to get another ride soon."

It seemed shabby not to give any explanation so Sarah said, "Thank you for the ride. I'm going to see my brother." Somewhat refreshed from her nap, she jumped from the wagon and reclaimed her meager possessions.

Relief settled over the old man's face. "That's good. Mighty good. There's nothin' like kinfolk." He took up the reins and clucked to the mules. "I better get along home. My old woman will be waitin' for me."

Sarah watched him until a bend in the side road hid him from sight.

Thank You, God, for sending him. I was so tired.

It wasn't the last time Sarah thanked God for providing for her needs. Other helpful people offered assistance and food. Sarah fought the dread of being overtaken every mile of the way, heartbeat quickening each time hoofbeats sounded behind her. She continued to be vigilant, but when no one showed undue interest in her cloaked, heavily veiled figure, she began to believe her goal of reaching California in one piece was actually possible. However, arriving in Jefferson City two weary days later convinced Sarah her arduous journey had just begun. She realized her only hope of reaching California before Judgment Day was to find a faster mode of transportation. Using extreme caution, her mouth dry from fear, Sarah wrapped her long dark veil around her head, bent forward and shuffled up to the ticket window in the Jefferson City train station like an aged woman. In a cracked voice she purchased a railway ticket to Denver. It was all the money she dared spend.

Once on the train Sarah remained wary of strangers and kept strictly to herself. Heart thudding she hid behind her veil each time the train stopped. She cast furtive glances at every man who boarded—and heaved great sighs of relief when she recognized no one and the train continued its journey.

In spite of keeping up her guard, the ever-changing landscape that rushed outside the train window fascinated Sarah. From cornfields to rolling hills and, at last, distant snow-covered peaks, it was unlike anything she had ever seen.

Sarah also comforted herself by rereading Seth's letters and reflecting on what a good man Matthew Sterling must be. She often lapsed into daydreams about meeting Seth's idol. Her heart beat fast beneath her worn traveling gown, and she blushed, remembering her fantasy about walking down the aisle of the Madera church to become Matt's bride.

"Why are you allowing a man you have never met to win a place in your heart?" Sarah chided herself. "Matthew Sterling is so far beyond your reach that it is foolish to allow him in your thoughts." Sarah sighed. Why couldn't Tice Edwards have been as honest and kind as Seth said Matt was? What a contrast! Despite reprimanding herself, every time Sarah looked at the faded photograph, she couldn't help wondering if God might be leading her toward happiness in the far West.

Yet scrunched up in her seat in the dark hours of the night, common sense mocked her. *Why would anyone as important as Matthew Sterling be attracted to a runaway girl whose education is limited to what her mother taught her and a love of books? A girl whose skills are better suited to drudging in Gus Stoddard's household than being mistress of a great ranch?* The cruel taunt plunged Sarah's spirits to the toes of her shabby shoes, but the coming of morning and whispering, "Get thee behind me, Satan," brought a measure of comfort.

The evening before the train reached Denver, Sarah sustained a terrible shock. When she took out her letters from Seth, she discovered one was missing! She felt the blood drain from her face. Impossible! Surely she would have noticed before now. She frantically searched her carpetbag to no avail. Her reticule. Her seat and the floor around her. Between the pages of her mother's Bible.

It was no use. The letter was gone.

Sarah tried to think what might have happened to it or where she may have lost it. A heartbeat later the truth hit her like two locomotives colliding head on. It painted a chilling picture in her mind. Once in the attic while musing and comparing Matt Sterling with Tice Edwards, she had been interrupted by the children swarming up the stairs, screaming for her attention. All Seth's letters and the photograph scattered to the floor. Sarah had hastily gathered them up and shoved them into her reticule.

Sarah swallowed the terror that threatened to overpower her and buried her face in her hands. *Lord, when I dropped the letters, one must have gotten pushed under my bed. Otherwise I would have noticed it my last night at home while I was frantically gathering my things.* What little sense of security she had been able to muster between spells of panic fled. Gus and Tice must know her destination, a truly alarming twist.

Sarah harbored no hope that they would give up and leave

her alone. Gus still had his debt. Tice had his pride. The owner of the *River Queen* would never stand for being made a laughingstock. By now all of St. Louis must be buzzing about Tice's being practically deserted at the altar. Any feelings he ever had for Sarah would have changed to hatred and the desire for revenge. Tice would never let her go. He and Gus would dog every step of her way until they found her.

Sarah groaned. When they did, Gus would swear on a stack of Bibles as tall as the snowcapped peaks of the Sierra Nevada that he was her legal guardian and had the right to return her to Missouri. The false documents he and Tice had illegally procured would convince the authorities. Her only hope was to reach the Diamond S before they caught up with her. Seth would fight to the death before allowing Gus and Tice to take his sister. And if Matthew Sterling was half the man her brother thought he was, he would protect her for Seth's sake.

During the remainder of the trip to Denver, every time the train stopped, Sarah shrank lower into her seat and fervently prayed. She asked just one thing: that she not look up and see Gus's ugly face leering at her. Or Tice Edwards's eyes filled with anticipation of the punishment he would surely inflict on the girl who hated him but would soon be in his power.

twelve

Denver, Colorado, at last.

Long before the train that carried Sarah Anderson away from a fate worse than death and into an unknown future reached the Mile-High City, she had gazed out the window in awe. Colorado was a far cry from St. Louis. Or the Great Plains. The rolling land ended abruptly at the foot of the mighty Rocky Mountains. Snowcapped peaks reached toward heaven and provided a spectacular backdrop for the city. Sarah rubbed her eyes to make sure she wasn't dreaming. An abundance of wildflowers added to the charm. *Thank You, God, for all this beauty. And for bringing me safe this far, even if I only have mere pennies left,* Sarah silently prayed.

Thoughts of her financial straits dampened the spirits that had soared at the grandeur of the Rocky Mountains. Sarah sighed and continued her prayer. *I'm less than halfway to Madera, Lord. Once I get off the train, I don't know where to go or what to do. Please help me.*

The monotonous *clackety-clack* of the train's wheels slowed. The grinding screech of brakes signified the "iron horse" would soon stop. Sarah gathered her meager belongings, leaving Seth's wooden pistol and her few valuables in her reticule. Should someone attempt to rob her, she could hang on to the reticule better than her heavy carpetbag. She stood and grimly muttered, " 'I will fear no evil: for thou art with me.' "

"Did you speak, miss?" the conductor asked.

Sarah felt herself redden. Although reticent about who she was and where she was going, she had found the white-haired conductor to be kind to her on the journey. Perhaps he would help her now. "I'm not familiar with Denver," she confessed. "Could you direct me to a boarding place for young ladies?"

The conductor's bushy white eyebrows rose almost to his cap. "A nice young lady like you shouldn't be running around alone," he advised. "Denver can sometimes be a rip-roarin' town." The eyebrows drew together. "Isn't anyone meeting you?" Disapproval oozed in every word.

"Not right away." Sarah fought back tears. It was true. Seth wouldn't be meeting her right away. More than a thousand miles lay between them. In the meantime she had to find a place to stay and some kind of employment.

The conductor's keen blue eyes reflected surprise before he gruffly said, "I take it you don't want any place fancy?"

Sarah nodded and swallowed the lump in her throat. Once she left the train and the kindly conductor, she would be on her own. No, not really alone. One person with God was a majority.

The conductor patted her on the shoulder and pulled a pencil and pad from his pocket. He wrote something, tore the page off, folded it, and wrote more on the outside. "I figured as much. Don't worry, miss. Take this to Miz Hawthorne's. This is her address. It's just a few blocks from here." He pointed. "She's a good Christian woman and will take care of you. If I had a daughter, my mind would be at rest if she lived at Miz Hawthorne's."

He paused then added, "It's best for you to put your veil over your face. Lots of first-rate folks here but some that ain't." He sent a significant glance at the crowded station platform. Sarah obediently pulled down her veil but choked up. "Thank you." It was like losing a friend when the conductor helped her down the train steps. He swung back up the steps, paused to wave at her, then disappeared into the railroad car that had come to feel like home. Clutching her reticule in one hand and her carpetbag in the other, she turned to face the station platform.

Sarah had run the gauntlet of admiring male eyes the few times she had been forced to visit the docks in St. Louis. Now, securely masked from curious stares by her heavy cloak and veil, Sarah thrilled at the sight of the men who lounged against the station walls: cowboys like she would find on the Diamond S. Some looked to be still in their teens. Garbed in checked or plaid shirts and high-heeled boots similar to those Seth and Matt Sterling wore in the picture Seth had sent, their hats looked wide enough to shade a city block. A few wore buckskins or woolly chaps. Sprinkled in the crowd gathered to meet the train were Indians in blankets and Mexicans in brightly colored clothing. A few women, who at first glance appeared not of her kind, stood nearby. Fewer children but several dogs.

Sarah took a deep breath. In spite of the warm day she pulled her cloak close around her, raised her chin, and briskly set out in the direction the conductor had pointed. Conscious of stares boring into her back, she felt grateful for the cloak that disguised her slender, girlish form.

When Sarah reached the hastily scrawled address, dismay filled her. Nothing at the white picket gate or on the door of the modest two-story white house indicated its owner took in boarders. Had the conductor been mistaken? Had "Miz Hawthorne" moved? If she still lived here, had she stopped welcoming strangers into her home? Sarah peered at the written address, wondering if she had misread it. No. The numbers matched those on the house.

Tired from travel and wanting to cry, Sarah considered leaving. She shook her head. Where could she go if she did? The house was obviously well cared for. Even if Miz

Hawthorne no longer lived there, surely whoever did could recommend a place where Sarah might find rest.

The weary girl resolutely opened the gate and walked up the flower-bordered path to the front steps and onto a hospitable, vine-clad covered porch. If only she could sink into one of the chairs that invited weary bodies to tarry! She couldn't. She must find safe shelter before nightfall.

Heart thumping, Sarah threw back her veil and knocked on the frame of the screen door. She noticed the inner door stood partly open. Good. At least someone was home. A moment later footsteps sounded. The inner door opened then the screen door, so quickly Sarah had to step back to avoid being struck. A round face framed with white hair and a cap that was askew appeared.

"May I help you?"

"I hope so," Sarah faltered. "Can you tell me where I might find Miz Hawthorne?"

Laughter bubbled up from deep inside the jolly woman. "I'm Miz Hawthorne, child. What can I do for you?"

"Do you still take in boarders?" Sarah clutched her reticule and carpetbag until her knuckles whitened. "There's no sign." She held her breath, hoping against hope she had found a refuge.

Blue eyes opened wide. "I've no need of a sign, dearie. Folks 'round here all know me. Besides, I don't take in just anyone. Only those my friends recommend." She cocked her head to one side. "Who sent you to me?"

Sarah sighed with relief. She dropped her carpetbag and searched in her reticule. "The conductor on the train. He said to give you this."

Miz Hawthorne barely glanced at the passport to her boardinghouse and tossed it onto a small table in the cool entryway. "Come in, come in, child. Welcome. Joseph wouldn't send me anyone who isn't all right. Lay off your wraps. I'll bring some cold lemonade."

Thank You, God, Sarah silently breathed. She removed her voluminous cloak, hat, and veil but wondered what the conductor had said to open the door of Miz Hawthorne's home so quickly. Sarah had scrupulously refrained from reading the note, but curiosity now overcame her. Feeling guilty she tiptoed to the table. With a furtive glance toward the door through which Miz Hawthorne had disappeared, she snatched up the missive. The message was short and to the point:

> *Here's a little lost lamb, Miz Hawthorne. Something's troubling her. Open your home and your heart. She can't pay much but needs help.*
>
> *Joseph*

Gratitude flooded through Sarah. A verse from Isaiah came to mind. *"And it shall come to pass, that before they call, I will answer; and while they are yet speaking, I will hear."* Even before she asked God to guide her as the train approached Denver, He had already prepared Joseph's heart to give aid when Sarah needed it most.

Over lemonade and cookies she threw caution to the winds and told Miz Hawthorne who she was and why she had fled St. Louis. "I'm down to almost nothing," she confessed. "I must find work. Do you know of anyone who can use me? I am strong and willing to do anything that's decent."

Miz Hawthorne shook her head. "I don't know of anything. If you're willing to help me out here, I can give you room and board, but that won't get you to California."

"I can sell my mother's wedding ring if I have to," Sarah told her. "But it's my last resort."

"Indeed it should be!" The old lady snorted. "Before you do

anything like that, let me see what I can find out."

A few days later, after Sarah had pounded the streets looking for work and found nothing, her landlady bustled into the kitchen where Sarah was finishing a mountain of dishes. She triumphantly waved a piece of paper. "A friend gave me the address of an employment office not far from here." She beamed. "There's a GIRLS WANTED sign in the window. Hurry yourself on over there before the positions are filled."

Sarah quickly changed from work clothes into her mother's Sunday-go-to-meeting dress. She plaited her red gold hair, wound the braids around her head, and topped them with her mother's old black hat. Heart beating with anticipation, she ran to within a block of the employment agency then slowed and regained her composure. It would never do to burst into an office red-faced and out of breath. "Please let the sign still be there," she murmured when she reached her destination.

It was. The door stood open. Should she knock or just walk in? Sarah had never faced this situation before so she tapped lightly and hesitated on the threshold. A masculine voice called, "Don't just stand there. Come on in."

A twinge of annoyance straightened Sarah's spine. A rather discourteous way to greet one. She lifted her chin and walked inside. Once she had a job, there would be no call for her to put up with such rudeness.

A well-dressed man about Tice Edwards's age sat with his feet propped on an untidy desk. He stared at her then stood. His belly bulged over a fancy, too-tight belt. "Well, and what have we here?" His teeth gleamed in the travesty of a smile. "Sit down. Sit down."

The look in his eyes reminded Sarah of Tice. It made her uncomfortable, but the need for a job overrode her desire to turn and run. She had outwitted a riverboat gambler. Surely she could put up with rudeness. Sarah poised on the edge of a chair facing the desk, still clutching her reticule. "I am looking for a position." It sounded better than *job*. "I can cook, sew, tend children, clean, or wait on tables."

The man looked her over and smiled again. "Take your hat off and let your hair down."

"I beg your pardon?" Sarah said in the icy voice with which she'd refused to marry Tice.

"Your hair. I can find you a better job than household drudge. The starting salary is—" He named what sounded to Sarah like a princely sum.

"What would I have to do, and why do you want my hair down?" Sarah demanded.

The man gave a long-suffering sigh. "Do you want a job, or don't you? You look like someone's sainted aunt with your hair like that. People who come to my club want to be served by girls who are lively and attractive. In the right clothes and with that hair, you can be a raving beauty. You'll make more just in tips than you can imagine."

A warning bell sounded in Sarah's brain. She remembered her father saying, *If something sounds too good to be true, it probably isn't true.* "Club? Do you mean a restaurant?"

He guffawed. "Hardly. I run the Golden Peaks Men's Club. High-class entertainment. Can you sing? Ace Hardin's girls have to do more than serve food and drinks." He leered. "A lot more."

Sarah stood so quickly that her chair crashed to the floor. She felt her face flame. "I will neither sing nor serve food and drinks in your Golden Peaks or any other club. Such places are unholy and lead men to destruction. They are an abomination to God and to decent people." She whipped around and started for the door.

Hardin sprang with the speed of a panther. He grabbed Sarah by the shoulders and kicked the door shut. "No one talks to Ace Hardin like that. You came in here of your own free will, missy." He began dragging her to an open door in the back of the room. "I'll lock you in the storeroom and let you reconsider. You're just the kind of girl who will bring customers to my place. I'm not passing up a chance like this."

Filled with horror Sarah slumped. Only Hardin's cruel grip kept her from falling. The next instant she began kicking and scratching with all her strength. She opened her mouth to scream, but Hardin let go with one hand and put meaty fingers over her mouth. "Shut up, you hellcat," he commanded.

It was the opportunity Sarah needed. She wrestled her right arm free and snapped open the reticule still hanging from it. She pulled out Seth's wooden gun and shoved the muzzle into the man's stomach so hard he let out a huge wheeze.

"Stand back!"

Hardin's mouth fell open. His skin turned a sickly green, and his hold on her loosened. "You—you're not going to shoot me, are you?" He took a step back.

Sarah pushed the gun farther into the overhanging belly that hid the carved pistol. "Put your hands in the air and walk backwards to the storeroom door," she ordered.

Step-by-step they crossed the room with Sarah's hand firm on Seth's toy. "Reach behind you, and open the door. Step inside and don't try any tricks. I won't say what might happen if you do." It wasn't a lie. If her bluff didn't work, she was a goner.

Hardin did as he was told.

The door closed behind him.

Sarah turned the key in the lock and fled from the employment office as if pursued by Gus Stoddard and Tice Edwards.

thirteen

When Sarah fled from Ace Hardin's employment office, she headed straight for Miz Hawthorne. She flung herself into the good woman's arms and sobbed.

"My goodness, child," the old lady gasped. "Whatever is the matter?"

"I should have left when I first felt something was wrong, but I need a job so much. I didn't know that he—" A fresh torrent of tears came.

Miz Hawthorne's arms tightened. "Who? What did he do to you?"

"He said to take down my hair and asked if I could sing." Fury dried Sarah's tears, and she sat up straight. "He said 'his girls at the Golden Peaks had to do more than serve food and drinks—a lot more. I told him such places were terrible and started to leave. He grabbed me and said he'd keep me in his storeroom until I changed my mind!"

"How did you get away?"

The absurdity of Sarah's escape sent her into peals of laughter. "I threatened him with a wooden pistol!"

"You *what*?" Miz Hawthorne stared as if she couldn't believe her ears.

Sarah chortled. "I really did." She groped in her reticule and brought out her weapon of defense. "I stuck the muzzle right in his fat belly and backed him into the storeroom. He thought I was going to shoot him!"

After a moment of stunned silence Miz Hawthorne said, "Well, I never!" and burst out laughing. When she could control herself, she wiped her eyes and pushed Sarah away. "We have to tell our sheriff about this right away. The idea, recruiting young girls to serve in such a place. The sheriff will put a stop to that."

"No," Sarah cried. "I'd have to sign my name on a complaint. It would become public knowledge. Please, Miz Hawthorne, don't tell anyone what happened." A new, terrifying thought struck her. "You don't know Tice Edwards. He has the chief of police in St. Louis under his thumb. If Gus found Seth's letter, Tice may already have had the authorities in St. Louis send telegrams to sheriffs along the train route." She finally convinced her landlady the best thing to do was for the runaway to lie low for a few days and see if there were repercussions from the fiasco, although Mrs. Hawthorne doubted there would be.

"I don't know this Ace Hardin, but if word ever got out that a slip of a girl had gotten the best of him with a toy pistol, the scoundrel would be the laughingstock of Denver." Her eyes twinkled. "After you leave, I'll tip off a deputy sheriff friend of mine. He's an honest young officer. If anything can be done to put Hardin out of business, he will see to it."

"You won't mention my name, will you?" Sarah pleaded.

"Oh no. I'll just say Hardin and the Golden Peaks Men's Club need looking into."

For the next week Sarah seldom went out, even to look for work. Miz Hawthorne guarded her as a mother cougar guards her cubs, and the few young ladies staying with her at the time knew nothing except that "Miss Joy" would soon be leaving. Yet Sarah no longer felt secure in Denver. Destitute and dependent on her landlady's kindness, the thought of being followed and dragged back to St. Louis against her will prompted her to forget about employment—especially after being nearly frightened to death when she saw a man who closely resembled Tice Edwards.

The next day she tearfully got out her mother's wedding ring and without a qualm gathered together the trinkets Tice brought while courting her and prepared to leave Denver. However, the pathetic amount she received from their sale left her without enough money for a quick ride to Madera. Although it would take much longer, she would have to make the last leg of her journey by stagecoach. Miz Hawthorne wanted to make up the difference, but Sarah refused.

"I won't be beholden to you, Mrs. Hawthorne. I can make it on my own the rest of the way. I have enough to purchase passage on the stage to Madera and pay for what little food I'll need and lodging at the stage stops. Once in Madera I'll be safe with my brother. The Diamond S Ranch is close by."

"I hate to see you go, child, but go you must," Miz Hawthorne told her. "Godspeed, and I'll be praying for you. Always remember: He cares for His own."

"I know." Sarah embraced her. "I'll never forget you. I'll send word when I get to California." *If you ever do,* an inner voice mocked.

Sarah didn't listen. God had delivered her from Gus Stoddard, from Tice Edwards, and from Ace Hardin. He knew what lay ahead and would prepare ways of escape.

ને

Sarah traveled the endless miles from Denver to Madera in a rocking coach. She shrank into a corner and looked over her shoulder at every stage stop. She kept her veil over her face much of the time, a shield against bold stares, even though it almost gave her heatstroke. She rejoiced when other women or families came aboard or clean-cut cowboys who glanced at her then respectfully looked away. If it became necessary to identify herself, she gave the name *Miss Joy*, which she'd used to take passage.

Not all the trip was unpleasant. Sarah marveled at the ever-changing landscape. Towering forests. Deep canyons with silvery streams rushing from their mountain birthplaces to their final destination: the Pacific Ocean. Huge rocks ranging from frowning granite walls to grotesque red peaks and columns. Stretches of desert with little shade. Pungent sagebrush. Giant tumbleweeds. Long-eared rabbits the loquacious driver called *jacks*. Deer and antelope. Sheep and cattle and horses.

Sarah learned from listening to California-bound ranchers who boarded the stage that there would be no sheep on the Diamond S. "Scourge of the earth," one weather-beaten man declared. "Those stinkin' sheep crop the grass so close our cattle starve, along with drivin' folks crazy with their *baa baa*."

Weary beyond description Sarah reached Madera travel worn and near penniless. She was tired of looking at flat land. Even glimpses of the snowcapped Sierra Nevada in the distance had palled—and if she never saw another stagecoach, it would be too soon. Thoughts of a real bath sent a pang of longing through her body. She sighed. Baths cost money she didn't have.

The stagecoach door swung open. Stiff from her long ride, Sarah carefully lowered her veil and accepted the driver's helping hand. She clutched her precious reticule and stepped out of the coach. The driver swung her carpetbag to the board sidewalk nearby. His team snorted and stamped, obviously eager to reach the large water trough in the middle of town. Their hooves stirred up a cloud of yellow dust. Sarah quickly reached for a handkerchief and held it over her nose, wondering what to do next.

The driver pointed toward the wooden sidewalk and a portly, bald man standing in front of a building identified as *Moore's General Store. Madera Post Office.* "Set yourself down in the shade of the store. Our postmaster will take care of you."

The jolly-looking man laughed. "I sure will, miss, or my name's not Evan Moore. Would you care for some lemonade? It's fresh made."

The friendly welcome unknotted Sarah's nerves. She threw back her veil, dropped to a bench, and fervently said, "I can't imagine anything I'd like more."

The postmaster's eyes twinkled. "Fine. Would you like to come inside or stay here in the shade? My 'post office' is actually just a cubbyhole behind the counter in my general store. It has enough pigeonholes for the mail."

Sarah smiled at him. "I'm too tired to move, Mr. Moore. If you don't mind, I'll see your post office—and the store—some other time."

"Fine. Fine." He rubbed his hands together and stepped inside. When he returned, carrying large glasses of cold lemonade, he sat down beside her. Sarah thanked him and timidly said, "I'm Sarah, Seth Anderson's sister. How can I get word to the Diamond S that I'm here?"

"Well, I swan! I shoulda known." Evan slapped his leg. "You resemble him some. Say, does he know you're coming?"

"No." Not sure how much to tell, Sarah said, "I wasn't sure when I'd arrive."

Evan scratched his bald head and looked troubled. "Last I heard, the Diamond S were driving the cattle up to the high country. I'm not sure when they'll be back. Do you want me to get someone to carry you out to the ranch?"

Bitter disappointment filled Sarah. What should she do? Except for a lone ten-cent piece, her coffers were empty. Pride warred with necessity—and won. "I can't just show up and beg to be taken in until Seth returns," she whispered.

"Any sister of young Anderson would be welcome on the Diamond S," the postmaster reassured her. "That's how we do things 'round here. By the way, call me Evan. Mr. Moore was my dad, God rest his soul. Anyway, if going to the ranch isn't to your liking, you bein' an Easterner and used to different ways and all, 'tain't no problem." He called to a freckle-faced boy kicking up dust with a worn boot, "You there, Johnny, get over here. This lady's Seth Anderson's sister. Ride out to the Diamond S, and tell them to send word to Matt and Seth that she's here."

Johnny grinned. "Sure, Evan. Whatever you say."

Sarah took the last of her money from her reticule and held it out. "Thank you, Johnny."

He drew back, and his face turned red. "Aw, you don't have to pay me. It's only ten miles."

How unlike the Stoddard children, Sarah thought. *This boy must be about Peter's or Ian's age but what a difference! Neither would walk across the street on my behalf, let alone take a hot, dusty, twenty-mile round trip without being well paid.* She pressed the dime in Johnny's unwilling hand. "Please. I'll feel better if you take it."

"Well, all right. Thanks." He pocketed the ten-cent piece and sped down the street toward the livery stable hollering, "Hey, Pa, I gotta ride out to the Diamond S. Seth Anderson's sister's here, and he don't know it. She's real nice, Pa—and purty."

Evan laughed outright, and Sarah felt warmed through and through. Never before had she been more aware of God's loving care and his promise in Isaiah: *"No weapon that is formed against thee shall prosper; and every tongue that shall rise against thee in judgment thou shalt condemn. This is the heritage of the servants of the Lord, and their righteousness is of me, saith the Lord."* God had cared for her every step of the way. Surely He would provide for her in this strange land that oddly enough didn't feel strange at all but as if she'd come home. She impulsively turned to Evan.

"Mr. Moore—Evan, I just gave my last dime to Johnny. I need a place to stay until Seth comes and a way to pay for it. It will take time for him to get back from the high country, won't it?"

"You can bet your bottom dollar on that. Don't fret, Miss Sarah." Evan stood and offered her his arm. "We'll just mosey on down to the Yosemite Hotel and see what the proprietor says. The captain took care of Seth when the boy was hurt. He thinks a powerful lot of him." Evan coughed. "We all do. Especially Matt Sterling. Seth reminds him of Matt's kid brother, who died a few years back."

If Sarah had been able to choose someone to enlighten her about Madera, she couldn't have found anyone better than Evan Moore. He proudly escorted Sarah to the Yosemite Hotel, talking while she observed. A wide main street, typical of other western towns she'd come through, stretched on either side of Evan's store and post office. The friendly man's face wreathed with smiles when he said, "We've got ourselves three hotels. Three general stores. A drugstore, a butcher shop, a blacksmith shop, and a livery." He laughed. "And according to Matt Sterling," he said impressively, " 'just about the prettiest and most wide-awake town in the entire San Joaquin Valley.'"

Sarah stifled a yawn. After the hustle and bustle of St. Louis, Madera seemed more sleepy than wide awake, but unwilling to offend she kept her opinion to herself.

After running out of information about the town Evan obviously loved, he said, "We've got some mighty fine folks here, Miss Sarah. Captain Perry Mace is one of them. He's been 'most everywhere and done 'most everything. Funny. The Mexican War's been over for ages, but he's never been called anything but 'the captain.' Wears a top hat all the time. Well," he added in a droll voice, "maybe not to bed."

Sarah rewarded him with a smile, but her heartbeat quickened. God sometimes led His children by strange paths. Would He use this eccentric adventurer to help her as he had helped Seth? It could be days before her brother was able to reach her.

On hearing Sarah's plight the captain promptly said, "Sho, you'll stay right here in my hotel until Seth comes." He waved an expansive hand. "You're more than welcome."

The kindness and western hospitality Sarah had encountered ever since she reached Madera brought a lump to her throat. She swallowed hard. "Thank you, sir. I appreciate it, but I will only accept on one condition. I'm no stranger to hard work and can earn my keep."

An approving look brightened the captain's keen eyes. "Spunky, just like that brother of yours. Good. If you want to work, it's fine with me. I can always use another girl to help wait tables." He glanced at her hot, dark traveling outfit. "You'll need a lighter dress though."

Would lack of proper clothing mean she wouldn't get the job? Even so, she had to be honest. "My few calico work dresses are pretty worn."

The captain waved aside her stumbling confession. "Your dress doesn't much matter as long as it is clean. The girls wear aprons that cover them from their necks to the tops of their shoes. I'll have Abby show you to a room and fix you up."

Sarah still wasn't satisfied. Even if she only worked for a few days, the captain must know the whole truth. "I've never waited tables, but I've cooked and scrubbed and taken care of a mean stepfather and his four ornery kids," she burst out.

"If you've done that, then I reckon you'll feel right at home waitressing." He shook Sarah's hand until her fingers tingled. "Thanks for bringing her over, Evan. Unless I'm a piker and not Captain Perry Mace, Miss Sarah's going to be a mighty fine gal to have around."

Several long, uncertain days passed with no sign of Seth. Although longing to see him, Sarah concentrated on her new job and quickly caught on. Her eagerness to always do more than her share endeared her to the other girls. It also won the captain's approval.

"I just wish I could keep you on permanently instead of just until your brother comes," he grumbled. "We're going into the busiest season of the year."

Sarah just smiled, but in the dark hours of the night, a daring thought took root in her mind and refused to be banished. *Why not keep working at the hotel after Seth comes?*

Another thought set Sarah's heart thundering. She wanted Matthew Sterling's approval as much as she'd ever wanted anything. If she kept her job, Seth would rage—but surely the hardworking rancher would respect and admire her a lot more than if she landed flat broke on the Diamond S.

fourteen

"That's the last of them, boys." Brett Owen's stentorian yell brought a roar of approval from the Diamond S cowboys. Grimy and tired from long days of chasing ornery cattle that preferred hiding in draws over being driven up to the high country, the thought of real beds instead of bedrolls on the hard ground gave Matt and his outfit reason to rejoice.

"First thing I'm gonna do when we get back to the ranch is sleep for a week," one of the hands announced. A murmur of assent rose, but Matt Sterling just laughed and turned to Seth Anderson.

"What's the first thing you're going to do?"

"Ride to Madera, and see if there's a letter from Sarah."

The poignant look in Seth's blue gaze hit Matt straight between the eyes. Ever since the telegram came from Gus Stoddard with the shocking news that Sarah had disappeared and might be on her way to California, Matt and Seth had waited in vain for word from the missing girl. Seth had grown quieter with each passing day. Matt's best efforts to cheer him up hadn't stemmed his worry—or Matt's.

"Gus and Tice won't give up," Seth said. "They'll hound her until they find her. I just pray to God it won't be before she gets here if she's coming. Once she does—"

Matt set his jaw. "Once she does, she's safe. Any trumped-up claim Gus Stoddard may have won't be worth a snap of his fingers. You're of age now and your sister's natural protector."

Some of the shadow left Seth's eyes, but Matt had more on his mind than Sarah's whereabouts. According to Gus's telegram, Sarah was engaged. The thought of the innocent girl tied for life to the kind of man her stepfather would choose made Matt grind his teeth. Yet how did he know she hadn't given her promise to marry? No. If she had, she wouldn't have run away.

Heedless of Seth's presence, Matt bowed his head. "Please help me, God," he prayed. "I love Sarah, but she's already committed to someone else. You've commanded that we should not covet our neighbor's house, his wife, or anything that belongs to him." Rebellion flared, and he burst out, "Surely that doesn't mean a Christian girl in danger of having her life ruined by marriage with a rotten, no-good polecat, does it?"

"Amen to *that*," Seth echoed.

Matt raised his head and clenched his hands. It took all his will to say, "Help me be honorable, Lord. May Your will be done in Sarah's life and in mine." But his traitorous heart silently added, *I hope Your will is for us to be together.*

⋙

The closer the outfit got to the Diamond S, the faster Matt's pulse beat. If only Sarah would write! She should have reached Madera by now—if that was her destination. Matt's spirits dropped to his trail-worn boots. Perhaps she had never left St. Louis. Perhaps friends had taken her in and hidden her. He shook his head. It didn't seem likely. As determined as Seth said Gus and Tice Edwards were, they'd have scoured St. Louis raw to find Sarah.

Hours later the outfit reached the Diamond S. The hands unsaddled and headed for the bunkhouse. Matt and Seth turned Chase and Copper out to pasture. Any riding into Madera for the mail would require fresh horses.

A small, colorful tornado burst from the ranch house door. "Senor Mateo. Senor Mateo." Solita ran to them, waving a wrinkled piece of paper. "Senorita Anderson is in Madera!

The message came more than a week ago." Tears glistened in her dark eyes. "The *muchacho* Johnny rode out the day the stagecoach bringing the senorita arrived."

Seth sagged against the corral fence. "Thank God!"

Matt silently added *Amen* then furiously said, "More than a week ago? Solita, why didn't you send word to the roundup?"

Wet streaks marred the housekeeper's smooth brown cheeks. "I myself ordered the lazy peon you hired just before leaving to take it to you. He said *si* and rode away. Only today did I find the paper by the barn. I pray to *Dios* that you will forgive me."

"Don't cry, Solita. It's not your fault."

She sniffled. "But where is Senorita Anderson? What must she think of us?"

A chill went down Matt's spine in spite of the hot day. "That's what we're going to find out." Matt wheeled and hollered to a stable boy. "Emilio, saddle two of our fastest horses. Pronto!"

Solita wiped her eyes with her voluminous apron. "Senor Mateo, shouldn't you take a buggy for the senorita? She may not be used to riding horses."

Seth laughed, the first real sign of mirth he'd shown since Gus Stoddard's telegram had arrived. "Sarah can ride. She had a chestnut gelding named Pandora before our father died. He had to be sold."

"Pandora for a *gelding*?"

Seth nodded and rolled his eyes. "That's what Sarah named him."

Matt chuckled but silently determined to search for the most beautiful chestnut gelding he could find. Sarah might be unwilling to accept it from him but would have no qualms if it came from Seth.

"We can get a horse for Sarah from the livery stable," Matt said. He ruefully looked down at his dust-encrusted garb.

"What say we clean up before going?"

Seth looked ready to mutiny. "You can if you want to, Boss. I'm going to find my sister."

His belligerence took Matt by surprise, but he nodded. "All right. It won't be the last time she will see trail dust." He followed Seth to the horses Emilio held and vaulted into the saddle. "Make tracks," he told his mount, and they headed for Madera.

The ten miles to town felt more like a hundred. Only Seth's excited chatter and the anticipation of meeting Sarah in person kept Matt from goading Chase into a full gallop. Would Sarah live up to her picture? Had her troubles taken a harsh toll on her spirit? More importantly could she ever feel the way about Matthew Sterling that he already felt about her?

At last they reached town. They permitted their horses to drink sparingly from the water trough then tethered them to the hitching post nearby. A moment later Evan Moore burst from the store/post office. "Where in blue blazes have you two been?" he yelled.

"Keep your shirt on," Matt snapped. "Where's S—Miss Anderson?"

"Workin' at the Yosemite Hotel. The captain told her she could stay until you came." He rubbed his glistening bald head. "She agreed only if she could work. She's been—"

Matt's and Seth's boot heels drummed on the wooden sidewalk and drowned him out. "Thank God she's safe," Seth muttered when they reached the hotel.

"Yeah. Now beat some of the dust off your jeans and wipe off your boots," Matt told him. "The captain runs a tight ship, and we look like a couple of scarecrows from a cornfield." Seth obeyed, then—heart thudding out of all proportion—Matt led the way into the hotel dining room.

He didn't need Seth's joyous cry, "Sarah!" to identify the

girl whose picture he carried. Her red gold hair lay braided across her head. Her lake blue eyes matched the sleeves of the sprigged calico gown peeping from beneath a white apron that enveloped her from the base of her neck to the top of her shoes.

Her heavily laden tray tipped and would have crashed to the floor if Seth hadn't sprung forward and caught it. "Seth. Oh, Seth!" The heartfelt cry and expression on her face told the story of what Sarah Joy Anderson had been through.

Seth laid the tray on a nearby table and wordlessly caught Sarah in his arms, but Matt hung back. Not for all the gold in California would he intrude on the long-delayed reunion. Instead, as skittish as a colt under his first saddle, he riveted his gaze on Sarah. Even the second photograph had not done her justice. She was the most beautiful young woman Matt had ever seen, with nothing but purity and honesty in her eyes. How different from Lydia's coquetry! Thank God, Sarah was nothing like the haughty girl who turned him down.

"Boss, this is Sarah," Seth said after what felt like an hour but was only a few minutes.

She extended a small, shapely hand and curtsied. "Mr. Sterling, I thank you for what you've done for my brother. I can never tell you what it means to me."

He smiled. "Call me Matthew. Or Matt. We're not much for 'Mistering' folks out here. Anyway, Seth carries his weight. You'll see how much when we get to the ranch."

"I'm sure I will when I come to visit." Her eyes sparkled. "And please call me Sarah."

"What do you mean, visit?" Seth sounded outraged "You're going home with us today."

"No. I've accepted a full-time position waiting tables for Captain Mace. The road to Yosemite has opened; the tourist season is in full swing. I can't impose further on your kindness, Mr. . .uh. . .Matthew. You've done enough for the Andersons, and I'm perfectly capable of making my own way."

Matt was shocked speechless. Not take Sarah to the Diamond S? His plans to have her close by and try to win her love hit the floor with a *thud*. He started to protest. Instead the question that had burned in his soul ever since Gus Stoddard's telegram arrived came out. "Sarah, are you promised in marriage?"

The next instant he felt like kicking himself to Fresno and back. But relief filled him when Sarah's eyes shot sparks and she said, "Promised? God forbid! Gus sold me to Tice Edwards to pay back six thousand dollars in gambling debts, but I never agreed to marry the scoundrel." Fear crept into her eyes. "I'm just afraid they will follow me. I dropped one of your letters, Seth."

Seth glanced at Matt and reluctantly admitted, "He sent word you had run away and—"

Sarah's face turned paper white. "He said he and Tice were coming, didn't he?"

Matt couldn't stand the agony in her sweet face. "Don't worry about it. Folks out here have a way of getting rid of varmints. If Gus and Tice come, Sheriff Meade and the Diamond S boys will kindly advise them this part of the country isn't healthy for St. Louis gamblers and their toadies."

Red flags flew in her cheeks. "Thank you. That makes me feel better. You can't know how hard it is to be alone with no one to help you."

"Come back to the ranch with us then," Seth insisted.

Sarah held her ground. No matter how hard Seth and Matt tried to talk her into staying at the Diamond S, she stubbornly refused.

Late that evening, after returning to the ranch empty-handed,

Matt headed for the rise overlooking his spread. The full moon hung over the range. Stars dusted the vast expanse. Cattle lowed in the distance, and the soft cries of night birds filled the still air. "Lord, Sarah is everything Seth said and more. I feel like I've been run over by a stagecoach." He threw his head back and laughed. "Just think. I once thought I was in love with Lydia Hensley!"

&

After Sarah saw Matt Sterling in person, she had more reason than ever to keep her job at the Yosemite Hotel. Her feelings of attraction had multiplied until she was secretly afraid to be near Matt on the Diamond S. Sarah knew she was falling deeper in love with the young rancher, but she didn't fully trust her feelings. Her experiences with Gus and Tice kept her wary of giving herself to someone she hardly knew, even in the unlikely event Matt could someday care for her. It was best for her to stay far, far away from him.

She did, however, accept enough money from Seth to buy some decent clothes. The capacious aprons covered a multitude of deficiencies, but Sarah felt self-conscious wearing gowns with frayed collars and cuffs. One of the general stores carried ready-made dresses, so she selected two lightweight work gowns and a white muslin for church. Her mother's dark blue was just too hot.

Sarah continued to make friends with her co-workers at the Yosemite, especially Abby Sheridan, who was a well of information about dark-haired, blue-eyed Matthew Sterling.

"He's truly the most eligible bachelor in the entire county, maybe in the entire valley," Sarah's new best friend said during a break between customers. "His character and principles are above reproach."

Sarah's heartbeat quickened. "It's sure good to know there are still honest men in the world," she replied. But when she heard Matt's praises sung over and over, against her will and common sense, Sarah began to daydream about the popular rancher once more.

One of the best things about working at the hotel was the opportunity for Sarah to live her Christian faith, planting seeds in the hearts and minds of her co-workers—especially Abby. Sarah's quiet but fun-filled personality soon made her a favorite with both regular customers and her fellow workers. At times she even forgot Gus and Tice.

Her idyllic world shattered whenever Red Fallon swaggered into the dining room. Matt had fired him after the spring roundup, tired of trying to keep him and Seth apart. In spite of being a top hand, Red was more trouble than he was worth.

Rumor had it that Red held a grudge against both Matt and Seth. It made Sarah shiver. From the first time Red saw Sarah, he dogged her steps. His bold gaze followed her every minute he was in the hotel dining room. He tried to walk with her on the street, paid her numerous compliments, and did all he could to get her to notice him.

Sarah actively disliked the obnoxious cowhand. She knew her rebuffs to Red's advances stung his pride, and she avoided waiting on him whenever she could. His biding-my-time look frightened her.

One Saturday after supper Sarah looked around the dining room and gave a contented sigh. The room was deserted. A medicine show had set up across the street from the hotel, and folks of all ages had hearkened to the *boom, boom* of the big brass drum.

She glanced out the window and smiled. The crowd looked tantalized by whatever entertainment the hawker was offering—probably an elixir that would cure everything from warts to summer complaint.

No matter, she thought. *The medicine show will allow me to finish my work earlier than usual.* Seth had promised to come see her, and she was looking forward to spending precious time with her brother.

"Go ahead," Sarah told Abby, who was helping her tidy up. "I'll finish here. I saw plenty of medicine shows in St. Louis and don't care about going."

"Are you sure?" Abby whispered with a pointed glance at Red, who was lounging in the doorway.

"Don't be silly," Sarah whispered back. "Bullies like Red waylay girls in alleys, not in hotel dining rooms. Besides—"

"Besides," Abby mimicked, "just maybe a certain Diamond S rancher will drop by like he often does on Saturday nights."

Sarah felt herself blush, but she laughed and retorted, "And just maybe you think my brother might be in town and at the show."

Her pretty, dark-haired friend grinned impishly. "Tit for tat. Thanks. I'll freshen up first." She disappeared through a side door into the hall, where a stairway led to the second-story rooms.

Before Abby's footsteps died away, Red strode into the dining room and started in with his usual effusive compliments.

Sarah ignored him. She took a deep breath and concentrated on a final tidying of her assigned tables. But she couldn't still her shaking hands.

"You and me oughta get hitched," Red insisted, coming up behind her. "No sense for a purty little gal like you to slave away here when you could be takin' care of me." He reached out and touched her shoulder.

Sarah whirled at his touch. She slapped Red's hand away and fixed him with a haughty gaze. "Keep your hands away from me, Mr. Fallon. I like my job here and intend to keep it. Now, get out."

Red's face turned a dusky red. "I'll teach you!" he raged. "Just like I'da taught your brother if Matt Sterling woulda kept his nose out of my business." He grabbed Sarah's shoulders and tried to pull her to him.

Biting pain and Red's reference to Seth and Matt freed Sarah from the horror of the moment. Horror she'd too often felt when Gus jerked her around. Fury gushed through her veins like water from a broken dam. Never again would Sarah allow any man to lay rude hands on her.

She jerked one arm free and swung at him with all the strength gained from hard work.

Crack!

The open-handed slap staggered Red and etched her fingerprints on his dangerously red face.

fifteen

Sarah's ringing slap was not meant for Red alone. The rage behind it was payback for the mistreatment she had received from Gus Stoddard.

Naked hatred sprang into Red's steel gray eyes. A curse made Sarah want to clap her hands over her ears. He lunged for her, arms extended and fingers curled into fists.

Sarah was too quick for him. She scurried around the table she'd just finished tidying. Regardless of the white cloth, shining cutlery, plates, bowls, and glasses set up for breakfast, she shoved the heavy table with all her might. It crashed into Red, hitting him in the stomach. He groaned and doubled over. His clawlike hands flew to his belly.

"How does it feel to be bested by a girl?" Sarah taunted. "You're a yellow coward and a bully, Red Fallon. No wonder Matthew Sterling fired you. After folks hear about this, you won't be able to get a job on any ranch in the valley." She regretted the words as soon as they left her mouth. Why hadn't she controlled her unruly tongue and kept still? The anger in Red's eyes showed he was not only obnoxious but downright dangerous as well.

"You wildcat!" He sprang around the overturned table but groped thin air.

Always quick stepping, Sarah knew her fury lent wings to her feet. *Why doesn't someone come? I need help.* Her heart sank. With all the commotion in the street, there was little likelihood anyone would hear the noise in the dining room. Sarah skipped behind another table and sent it flying.

Red stepped out of the way. Before she could barricade herself again, his long legs strode toward her. His face darkened into an ugly scowl. He let loose a string of oaths reminiscent of Gus Stoddard at his worst. Then he backed Sarah against the wall. When she tried to scream, Red put a huge paw over her mouth and gloated at her futile attempts to free herself. Triumph shone in his contorted features. "I've got you now!"

Never had Sarah known such terror, not even when she faced down the saloon owner in Denver with Seth's wooden pistol. Her slender frame was no match for the hulking cowhand.

❧

Earlier that afternoon Matt Sterling and Seth Anderson rode in from the range and dropped into comfortable chairs on the shady ranch house porch. Seth grinned. "Sure feels good to sit on something softer than Copper!"

"Or Chase." Matt stretched and yawned, glad for the chance to relax. "We rode farther than we'd planned." He glanced toward the west. "Sun's going down in a hurry this evening."

Seth bounded to his feet.

"What's the trouble?" Matt asked, suppressing another yawn.

"I promised Sarah I'd ride in and see her today." Seth replied, shamefaced. "I've gotta clean up and get to town."

Matt searched for an excuse to go along and fell back on the tried and true. He stood up and said, "Think I'll mosey along with you and get the mail."

"Glad for the company." A grin spread across Seth's face. "Won't be surprised if Sarah will be, too." With a mocking laugh he headed off to get ready, leaving Matt with his mind miles away.

When Matt and Seth reached town, they watered their horses and hitched them to the rail in front of the Yosemite

Hotel. Matt shook his head in amusement at the crowd of folks gawking at the medicine show.

"Nice weather brings the hawkers out more than usual," he commented. He fell in step with Seth as they climbed the porch stairs to the hotel.

"I thought you were going for the mail," Seth reminded him.

"Plenty of time for that," Matt replied sheepishly.

The two men stepped into the hotel's dining room and stopped short. The room looked like it had come through a war. Overturned tables, cutlery, smashed dishes, and glasses littered the floor.

"What's carrying on in here?" Matt thundered, scanning the debris.

A muffled shriek drew his attention across the room. His eyes widened in horror. *Sarah!* And Red! The rough cowhand had Sarah backed against the far wall and was shaking the living daylights out of her.

Seth gave a low groan and leaped for the pair.

Matt yanked Seth back. Roaring, he flew over the tables and dealt a hard left to Red's jaw. Then he tossed him halfway across the room with one powerful heave. Red lay unmoving where he landed. Was the ruffian dead? At that moment Matt didn't care.

"Oh Matt, thank God you're here!"

Sarah's agonized cry sent an arrow straight to Matt's heart. He reached her in a single bound and knelt beside her, wishing he had the right to hold her close.

The thud of heavy boots heralded Seth's approach. "Sarah, are you all right? Did that lowdown skunk hurt you?" Without waiting for an answer he jerked his chin at Red. "Is he dead?"

"Naw, I ain't dead." Red groggily sat up and rubbed his jaw.

Blue murder flashed in Seth's eyes. "If you've hurt my sister, you will be!" He sprang toward Red, hands balled into fists.

Matt leaped up and restrained the young man for the second time. "Let's leave Red for the law." His quiet command halted Seth's progress, but it didn't restrain Seth's tongue.

"Red Fallon, I'm gonna nail your ugly hide to the barn door if you ever get near Sarah again," he threatened.

"And I'll hand him the hammer and nails!" Matt paused. "That's not all. One more stunt like this, and we'll sic the Diamond S on you. Brett and the boys think a powerful lot of Sarah. They've had a craw full of you and your shenanigans. Some of the outfit's already rarin' to take a piece out of your hide." Matt's voice grew deadly. "I can't rightly say I could stop them if they made up their minds to have a necktie party—with you as the guest of honor."

"Yeah," Seth Anderson put in. "There's this big ol' cotton-wood just out of town. A great place for a hanging."

Red's face turned a sickly yellow. He reached for his gun, but Matt nimbly kicked it out of his hand. "Seth, go fetch Sheriff Meade." Matt knew he'd better keep his young friend as far away from Red Fallon as he could for now.

❧

From her position across the disturbed room, Sarah felt torn between relief that the sheriff would come soon and a horrid fascination with the explosive situation. Did Matt and Seth mean the cowboys would *hang* Red? Seeing their wrath, she believed it could happen. Even in the short time she had been in Madera, Sarah had learned about the code of the West. The unwritten law carried harsh consequences. According to articles in the *Expositor* newspaper, it could even mean a death sentence for men who insulted decent girls and women as Red had insulted her.

"Not all the varmints out here are four-legged," Abby had warned. "The code of the West is what protects girls like you and me from the two-legged kind."

A new thought struck Sarah. Would Matt and Seth's Christian principles, especially the commandment *Thou shalt not kill,* be able to deter the two men she loved if Red transgressed again?

Will yours, an inner voice demanded, *when the pain Red inflicted and the fear of it sometime happening again make you want to shout, "Hang him! I'll get the rope!"*

Sarah had been angry and helpless when Gus ill-treated her, but she'd never wished him dead. Now the realization of what she was capable of thinking appalled her. For the first time she realized the wickedness of feelings generated by hate. Feelings she wouldn't have dreamed possible lurked beneath her calico gown.

Jesus, forgive me. You said, "Whosoever hateth his brother is a murderer: and. . .no murderer hath eternal life abiding in him." I am so sorry!

Sick at heart from learning what lay hidden in her soul, Sarah was still aware when Sheriff Meade arrived and handcuffed Red. She roused from her misery when the sheriff said, "You can cool your heels in jail, Red. This time you've gone too far." He wheeled toward the distraught girl. "I'll need you to sign a statement, Miss Sarah. Once you do, this skunk won't bother you again. There's not a jury in the state that won't hand down a guilty verdict when they hear how he roughed you up."

The vision of a lifeless figure hanging from the limb of a cottonwood tree made Sarah shudder. She licked suddenly dry lips. If a jury sentenced Red to death, he would leave this world and enter into a greater punishment than she could bear, no matter how much he deserved it. "Just make him go away," she whispered. "I don't want his blood on my hands."

Seth gave a murmur of protest, and Sheriff Meade's

eyebrows shot skyward. "You won't press charges?"

She mutely shook her head.

"But Sarah—"

"No, Seth. Let him go." She looked from her brother to Matt, who stood as if turned to stone. His dark blue gaze bored into Sarah. She unflinchingly met it, knowing he held Red's life in his hands. Even if she didn't press charges, Matt's testimony of what he had seen would condemn the cowboy. A minute passed. Two. Sarah's heart pounded like cannon fire.

What felt like an eternity later, Matt took a ragged breath and whirled toward Red. "She's saved your bacon, Fallon. Get out of the valley, and don't come back."

Some of the color returned to Red's face. He rubbed the darkening bruise on his jaw and silently stalked out past the sheriff, leaving Sarah haunted by his venomous look. It shouted more clearly than words: *This ain't over. Not by a long shot.*

◈

Summer passed, then September. Although vigilant as ever, Sarah began to relax. There had been no sign that Gus or Tice was anywhere in the area. Red had mercifully disappeared, at least for the time being. Sarah liked her job, her co-workers, and especially the warmhearted Captain Mace. She felt she had found a home in Madera.

Matt Sterling dined at the hotel more often than he did at home. Soon the entire town suspected he had fallen for pretty Sarah Anderson. She endured the teasing from her fellow workers, yet the blush that colored her cheeks each time the faithful customer entered the dining room was more than mere embarrassment. So was the swift beating of her heart when Matt sat down at her table. The only real embarrassment was the size of his tips. Sarah finally accepted an invitation from Matt to walk her home from church services one Sunday. Just maybe it would be God's plan that she become part of Matt's life.

Late that fall while the Diamond S crew was out rounding up strays, shots rang out and Seth slumped over in his saddle. He had been seriously wounded by an unknown assailant. Matt thought his heart would break when Brett and the boys packed Seth in. *Oh God, please save him,* Matt prayed. *This is like losing Robbie all over again. How can I tell Sarah? I'm responsible for her brother. She trusted me to take care of him. Now Seth may die because he's working for me. Even if this is Red Fallon's revenge, it can't be proved. No one's seen hide nor hair of Red in weeks.*

Seth's injuries were so dangerous that when Doc Brown arrived from Madera and examined the young man, he flatly stated, "He's in no condition to be moved to town. The trip would kill him. Go get his sister. He needs to be cared for here."

Dreading the confrontation with Sarah, Matt rode as he had never ridden before. When he reached the Yosemite Hotel, he told Captain Mace what had happened and asked him to summon Sarah. Her puzzled expression when she entered the office quickly changed to fear when Matt said, "I have some bad news. Seth has been. . ." He paused and considered his words. "Hurt," he finished.

Her lips quivered then set in a straight line. "How badly?"

"Enough for you to take a leave of absence and come out to the Diamond S to help Solita and me care for him," he told her bluntly.

Captain Mace wholeheartedly agreed. "The road to Yosemite will be closing soon for the winter, so I won't need you. Take good care of Seth. Your job will be waiting for you when you return in the spring."

If she returns, Matt thought. *If I have my way, Sarah Joy*

Anderson will be Mrs. Matthew Sterling by the time the road opens again. He wisely kept his thoughts to himself. With Seth so badly hurt, this was no time to openly pursue Sarah.

"It won't take me long to pack," she said. "I can't wait to see Seth. He's not going to die, is he?" Terror darkened her blue eyes.

Matt wouldn't lie, so he merely said, "He's sure to get better when he sees you," and let it go at that.

&

On the way to the ranch Sarah hunkered down in the carriage and announced, "I will earn my keep by helping Solita when I'm not needed to nurse Seth. That's how it's going to be. Period." The tilt of her sturdy chin showed she meant what she said.

"Did anyone ever tell you you're as stubborn as a mule?" Matt asked. To his amazement Sarah burst out in a chime of laughter that made the high-stepping horses' ears prick up.

"Oh yes—a *Missouri* mule!"

Matt grinned, outwitted and more in love than ever. God willing, that was where she would always be: close beside him for the rest of their lives.

sixteen

A pall lay over the Diamond S equal to when first the elder Sterlings then young Robbie died. Now Seth Anderson's life hung in the balance. Everyone on the ranch had learned to admire and respect the plucky tenderfoot who made good. Under the capable direction of Brett Owen, life went on but not as usual. The outfit walked softly, hoping and praying for Seth but knowing how little likelihood there was of him recovering. One of the bullets that felled Seth had lodged close to his heart. The ranch held its collective breath until Doc Brown dug it out.

The rejoicing was brief. The operation took far longer than even Doc Brown expected. Seth pulled through but remained unconscious. The shock of the surgery to his body and the loss of blood he'd sustained had left him so weak even Sarah wondered if he would live. Once the doctor operated—ably assisted by Matt and Solita, with Sarah hovering outside the bedroom-turned-operating room—Sarah refused to leave Seth's side. Only when her body refused to keep vigil and forced her to her room for a few hours of uneasy sleep would she desert her post.

Haggard from worry, Matt faithfully remained on duty as well. He and Sarah spent hours with Seth, asking God to spare the life of the boy they loved. They soon noticed Seth's fingers stopped plucking the sheets at the sound of their voices in prayer. "Try quoting scripture to him," Matt suggested.

Sarah again blessed her parents for instilling in their children the truths of the Bible. If Seth could hear her voice, he would surely recognize the verses, perhaps even receive comfort from them. Besides, Doc Brown admitted no one knew how much an unconscious person grasped.

"I've read about cases where patients came out of a coma and repeated things they'd heard, even when they couldn't speak," he gruffly told them. "Anything that quiets Seth is good."

So while her brother hovered close to death's door, Sarah held his hand and quoted scriptures, praying they would reach through the curtain that kept Seth from awakening.

"In the world ye shall have tribulation: but be of good cheer; I have overcome the world.

"Let not your heart be troubled: ye believe in God, believe also in me.

"Peace I leave with you, my peace I give unto you. . . ."

When Sarah's voice threatened to give out, Matt took over. The weary girl rested her head on one hand and let the stories of those whom Jesus had made whole flow over her like a healing stream. She prayed for Seth to hear them—especially the story where Jesus commanded the man with the palsy to take up his bed and walk.

Matt finished reading, bowed his head, and said, "Lord, we know that You love Seth even more than we do." He reached across the bed and took Sarah's hand in one of his own. "We ask You to spare our brother's life." He paused, as if struggling to go on. When he did, his voice broke. "Nevertheless, Thy will, not ours, be done." The last word was barely audible.

Sarah felt a lump the size of a windmill leap to her throat. The agony in Matt's voice showed how much it cost him to relinquish Seth into God's care. *Matt is stronger than I am,* she thought. *Seth is my sole remaining link to our once-happy home. I'm sorry, God, but I just don't want You to take Seth. He's all I have left.*

Sarah's confession brought relief, but she added, *If it is Your will, Lord, please make me willing to accept it. That's as far as I can go right now.*

Seth lingered between life and death for several more days. Then one afternoon, the overworked Doc Brown told Matt, Sarah, and Solita, "He's going to make it. His fever's gone, and he shows signs of regaining consciousness. Don't thank me," he barked when Sarah started to speak. "I'm just a rough old sawbones. The Almighty had a hand on Seth, or he wouldn't still be alive. I've a sneakin' hunch all the prayin' and readin' from the Good Book did their part, too."

Doc cleared his throat and shook a bony finger at the three. "Once awake, Seth will want to get up. Keep him in bed if you have to hog-tie him! He's going to need the same watchin' over he's been getting."

Too overcome with hope and joy to reply, Sarah felt tears of relief spill down her cheeks.

Not so for Matt and Solita. Matt's quick "Don't worry, he'll get it" was drowned out by the Mexican housekeeper's fervent "*Dios* be praised! I will care for Senor Seth the way I cared for Matelito and Dolores." A flood made glistening tracks down her round brown face.

"You'll probably spoil him rotten," Matt told Solita. His obvious attempt to lighten the moment and drive away the shadows that lurked in Sarah's eyes brought a look of gratitude and a small smile. How would she have lived through the ordeal without him?

"No wonder Seth idolizes Matt," she told herself after Doc Brown ordered her away for a sorely needed rest. She fell into the deepest, most refreshing sleep she had known since she arrived at the Diamond S and didn't awake until Solita shook her hours later.

"Come quickly, senorita." The housekeeper's face shone like

a brown full moon. "Dios is good. Senor Seth is awake!"

Sarah sprang from her bed and barreled into Seth's room. Matt stood by the bed, one hand on her brother's shoulder. "Don't try to talk," he advised the groggy young man. "You were shot. God and Doc took care of you. Now you need to rest. There's plenty of time to talk later."

Seth looked from Matt to Sarah. A wan smile crossed his pale face, and his eyes closed again. But Sarah dropped to her knees beside his bed and thanked God.

With the good news about Seth, joy descended on the ranch like rain from heaven. The Mexican workers played their guitars and sang again. The cowboys let off steam in a dozen different ways: playing tricks on one another and bragging, "Sho, we knew all along that Seth wouldn't die from any ol' bullet. He's too tough to let a little thing like that get him down."

Their antics delighted Sarah and showed better than anything else could have done in what high esteem the outfit held her brother.

Seth grew stronger with each day. For the first time, Sarah had time to appreciate the ranch. Compared with life in St. Louis, Sarah had considered living in Madera close to heaven. Now she discovered life on the Diamond S was even better. She fell in love with everything about the ranch: the grinning cowboys who surreptitiously eyed her then blushed when she caught them; the dark-eyed vaqueros; the horses in the corral; the distant Sierra Nevada. Most of all, Solita. Sarah loved listening to the housekeeper's warm tales of Matt's little sister, Dori, and his brother, Robbie.

One day Solita rolled her expressive eyes and pounded down a huge mound of bread dough. "Dolores means *sorrowful*. She brings sorrow to those who displease her or stand in the way of what she wants. She is not bad," Solita hastily added, 'just filled with mischief. I am to blame. She is like my own muchacha and so beautiful it is hard to deny her anything." She sighed, and her hands stilled. "Dori saw an advertisement in a magazine for Brookside Finishing School for Young Ladies in Boston. She pleaded and cried. I reminded Senor Mateo that Senora Sterling would be glad for her daughter to attend such a school." Solita sighed. "He spent much money getting a place for her, and I almost wished I had not urged him to do so. Our casa seemed empty until Senor Seth came. Then Senor Mateo and I, we laugh again." She shot a keen look at Sarah and innocently added, "He also laughs much now that you come to California, senorita."

Sarah felt a blush rise from the modest neckline of a sprigged cotton dress she had bought in Madera. She fingered the crisp white trim on the cuffs and quickly changed the subject. "I would have loved to go to such a school," she said in a small voice. Hating the "poor me" tone of her voice, she asked, "Does Dori like it there?"

Solita grunted. "Who can say? She would be too proud to admit it if she does not." Solita lowered her voice. "Dori has been in what Senor Mateo calls 'scrapes.' It is a wonder she has not been sent home in disgrace. I think Senor Mateo has had to pay *mucho dinero* to keep her there." Sarah saw how disturbed the housekeeper was over Dori, so she said, "Tell me about Robbie, please."

"It is a sad story. He wanted to prove he could do everything Senor Mateo did—but Roberto was too young." She sighed. "I think Senor Mateo's heart broke in two pieces when Roberto died."

Sarah couldn't hold back a question she'd wanted to ask for a long time. "Did no one try to heal it?" She felt guilty for asking but blurted out, "The girls at the Yosemite Hotel said

Matt had been engaged to a girl named Lydia Hensley. . . ." Her voice trailed off.

"Si." Solita's face clouded up like the sky before a thunderstorm. "That one was no good." She pounded her dough again as if taking out her disgust with Miss Hensley. "Senor Mateo vowed to never again trust a girl or woman. Senorita, he kept that vow until he saw your picture."

Sarah sat bolt upright. Heat raced through her veins. "What do you mean?"

"It is true. Senor Seth told me that since he gave the picture to Senor Mateo, it has ridden in Senor Mateo's shirt pocket."

Sarah couldn't doubt Solita. So Matthew Sterling carried her picture. Did he look at it as often as she did the one she had of Seth and him? She gulped. "I don't understand. Why would Seth give him my picture?"

Solita quietly said, "Both senors were worried about you and praying for you. We all were." The sweetest smile Sarah had seen since her mother died brightened Solita's face. "Every day I say *gracias a* Dios, thanks to God, who brought you safely to us."

Sarah knew she'd be bawling if she didn't get away. She hugged the diminutive housekeeper and escaped from the kitchen—but not from the effect of Solita's disclosure. Imagine. The girl-shy Matthew Sterling carrying her picture!

A few days later Matt stunned Sarah by presenting her with a beautiful chestnut gelding.

"Why, he looks just like Pandora, the horse of my childhood," she cried in delight. "Seth must have had a hand in the selection. But I can't take him."

"Of course you can. He's a gift from Seth and a bribe from me," Matt told her.

"What kind of bribe?" Sarah suspiciously demanded.

"You need to get out of the ranch house and into the fresh

air and sunshine to keep healthy," Matt said. "Not just for your own sake but for Seth's. You've been cooped up too long. Now that he is recovering, you have to think of yourself. You've gotten thin and peaked looking. A good dose of the outdoors is just what the doctor ordered. You'll also have more to tell Seth when you get back."

"Did Dr. Brown ask you to take me riding?" Sarah held her breath and waited.

"Hardly!" Matt's eyes lit up. "My own idea, but I'm sure he'd have prescribed it if he'd thought of it."

The afternoon rides quickly became part of Sarah and Matt's routine. While Seth napped, was pampered by Solita, and grew strong, Sarah and Matt explored the vast holdings that made up the Diamond S. She loved every inch of the place.

Late one golden October afternoon Matt took Sarah to his special place overlooking the ranch. The promontory offered both privacy and beauty. The entire valley spread out before them, with its vineyards and orchards, its cattle and horses. They dismounted and gazed down into the valley for a long time. Sarah passionately wished she could stay there forever.

Matt wheeled from the view. He drew Sarah close in his strong arms. "I love you, Sarah Joy Anderson," he said. "I want you to marry me and never leave the Diamond S. You don't need to answer right away, but no one on this earth can ever love you as much as I do."

Shaken by his intensity and the beauty of the moment, Sarah longed to respond to the gentle invitation in his eyes. She hesitated then faltered. "Matthew, I admire and respect you with all my heart, but. . ."

"But you don't know if you love me." Disappointment cast a shadow over his strong features, but it vanished the next moment. "I'll settle for your admiration and respect—for now—and leave the future in God's hands. Don't worry about it." He leaned forward and kissed her forehead. "I understand."

Sarah felt torn. How could he understand when she didn't? Before she pledged herself to this fine man, she must settle something forever: Were her feelings really love? Or were they hero worship mixed with gratefulness for everything he had done for her and Seth? She must be sure. "I need time to think," she whispered.

"Take as long as you need," Matt offered. He released her and raised an eyebrow. "I can afford to be patient. I intend to live to be an old, old man." His eyes sparkled. "I'll bet my bottom dollar that someday you're going to walk up the aisle of our Madera church on Seth's arm, all gussied up in a fluffy white dress and ready to become Mrs. Matthew Sterling."

Sarah gasped and stared at him. Impossible as it seemed, the scene Matt described was identical to the one she had conjured up while being fitted for the hated wedding dress months before—the dress Tice Edwards had paid for but had never seen her wear.

seventeen

Now that Seth was rapidly improving, Sarah's worries should have been over. They weren't. She was faced with a dilemma that had nothing to do with her brother's health. Captain Mace had promised she could return to waitressing at his hotel, but his trade depended heavily on the Yosemite Stage and Turnpike Company, which daily transported tourists from Madera to the Yosemite Valley. The visitors remained overnight before returning home the following day. The stage line, however, had ceased operation for the year and would not resume until spring. This meant that the captain could only keep a limited number of girls working during the winter, and Sarah was the newest employee.

On a beautiful Indian summer morning while Matt and the boys were busy away from the ranch house, Sarah saddled the chestnut gelding she had already learned to love and rode out alone. John Anderson had taught his daughter well, insisting that she learn to saddle and care for the first Pandora before he allowed her to even ride to the borders of their small farm.

Riding Pandora II brought back so many happy memories! Sarah giggled, remembering the look on her father's face when she announced she wanted to name her new horse Pandora. A twinkle crept into his blue eyes, and his lips twitched.

"Pandora?" He scratched his head and looked puzzled. "Seems to me Pandora was not only a gal but one who caused a heap of trouble. She opened a box she'd been told not to and let loose a passel of evil on the world—including sickness. Are

128

you sure you want that name?"

Sarah stubbornly shook her head. "No. It said in a book that Pandora means *all gifts*, and he's a gift. Besides, my horse wouldn't ever do anything bad. It doesn't matter if he has a girl's name."

"Then Pandora it is," John Anderson said. "You are responsible for taking care of him. That means feed, water, muck out his stall, brush, and curry him."

"I will, Pa."

Sarah had faithfully kept her promise until the awful day she watched a stranger mount the gelding and ride away. "If Pa had lived, we would never have had to sell Pandora," Sarah told her mother.

"I know." Mama looked as sad as Sarah felt. "We can't stay on the farm. It no longer belongs to us. You know we need the money to get to St. Louis."

"I know, but Seth gets to keep Copper!"

"Would you have me sell Copper in order to keep Pandora?"

Sarah felt ashamed. Seth had raised Copper from the time he was weaned. Selling him would almost be like selling Seth. "No, but I will miss Pandora *so much*."

"We all will." Mama hugged Sarah. "Someday if we have enough money, I hope you can have another horse."

Now, years later and nineteen hundred miles from the farm, Sarah had another Pandora. A wave of gratitude toward Matthew Sterling flooded through Sarah's body. "Lord, what would Mama and Pa think of me now?" she prayed. "And of Seth?" Love for the brother whose life God had spared settled into Sarah's heart. How could she help loving Matt when he had been so good to Seth and her?

"That's the problem," she told Pandora. "He's everything I ever dreamed of, but I have to be sure of my feelings. I don't want to marry Matt out of gratitude. Or because I see him as the answer to my worries about Gus finding me. Or being forced to wed Tice. It wouldn't be fair to either of us." A new and horrid thought rushed into her mind.

"I didn't actually read the papers Gus waved at me." A chill went through her. "What if Gus had copied Mama's handwriting and wrote a letter naming him as my legal guardian in case anything happened to her?"

The thought was so appalling that Sarah nudged the gelding into a canter in order to escape. Pandora settled into the easy stride that ate up distance like a visiting preacher gobbling down fried chicken. At the foot of the hill that sloped up to the promontory offering solitude—Sarah's favorite thinking place—Pandora slowed for the climb, but he wasn't even winded when they reached the top.

Sarah loved the spot for itself and not just because she had spent happy times here with Matt. Nothing disturbed the quiet except the sound of cattle lowing in the distance, the occasional cry of a hawk, Pandora's occasional gentle whinny, and a breeze rustling through the manzanita. A carpet of needles beneath a pine offered a soft place to rest and ponder knotty problems.

Sarah sat down and clasped her hands around the knees of her divided riding skirt. No sidesaddle for her. Back on the farm, she'd ridden in Seth's britches when they got too small for him.

However, Solita had raised her eyebrows in horror at the idea and produced a riding skirt Dori had left behind when she went back east. "Senor Mateo would not like you to dress so," she protested when Sarah came into the kitchen clad in trousers and ready for her first ride with Matt. "Senorita will wear this. *Mucho mejor.* Much better."

"Didn't Dori ride in pants?" Sarah asked.

The corners of Solita's mouth turned down. "Only when

Senor Mateo was not here to stop her."

Sarah snatched the skirt and went to her room to change. From then on she scrupulously dressed to go riding according to Solita's decree.

Sarah always felt close to God on the promontory. It offered the opportunity to seek Him and lay her concerns at His feet. The hustle and bustle of a busy ranch didn't always offer the opportunity to be alone and quiet. She had always treasured the scripture *"Be still, and know that I am God."* Nowhere else could she find a better setting to obey His command.

Today another verse came to mind. The advice from James was as applicable for Sarah as for those to whom they were originally directed: *"If any of you lack wisdom, let him ask of God, that giveth to all men liberally, and upbraideth not; and it shall be given him. But let him ask in faith, nothing wavering. For he that wavereth is like a wave of the sea driven with the wind and tossed."*

Sarah pondered the timeless admonition then stared unseeingly across the valley. "Lord, I thank You for bringing me to this place. I thank You for Your loving care and that Gus and Tice have not followed me. Yet I feel they will come. Neither will give me up without a fight." She shivered and hugged her knees tighter.

"In the meantime I need a job. Should I go to Fresno and look for work? It's a much bigger town, and Captain Mace will surely give me a good recommendation." She shook her head, and dread crept from the tip of her toes to the crown of her head. "I don't know anyone in Fresno. I would have to pay for my room and board. If Gus and Tice come, I'll have no one to protect me." She hastily added, "You can, of course, but is it really Your will for me to leave the Diamond S?"

Emotion surged through her. Leave Seth? Matt? Solita? The cowboys who respectfully tipped their Stetsons to her when she passed by? This promontory where she felt God's presence in every stirring breeze, every bird's song? No—yet how could she stay? If only there was something she could do at the ranch.

"I'll be glad to do any kind of work, Lord," she promised. "I just don't know what. When I try to help Solita, she shoos me away and tells me to go amuse Senors Seth and Mateo. The maids who help her giggle and shake their heads when I offer to make beds or dust. It feels like a conspiracy."

She jumped up, smoothed out her riding skirt, and mounted Pandora. "Do you know what I am going to do, my fine, four-footed friend? I am going to tell Matt Sterling point-blank that either he puts me to work, or I'll go where I can work."

With a prayer in her heart that she wouldn't have to leave, Sarah left her trysting place and headed home—the first real home she and Seth had known since their father died.

⁂

God answered Sarah's prayer in a way she wouldn't have suspected if she lived to be older than Methuselah. That same evening, Matt, Seth, Solita, and she gathered in front of the huge rock fireplace in the spacious ranch house sitting room. Dancing flames turned Seth's hair to glistening gold. The crackling fire targeted the brilliant colors of the beautiful Mexican tapestries on the walls and glinted off the silver belt buckle Seth sat polishing.

Sarah took a deep breath. It was time to state her own little declaration of independence. "I need a job."

A stick of dynamite exploding in the quiet room couldn't have had a more startling effect. Solita's mouth dropped open. Seth stared then burst into a loud "Haw haw!"

Matt sat up straight in his hand-hewn chair and gave Seth a quelling look. "What would you like to do, Sarah? I have enough cowhands. You're a good rider, but I don't think you could tame wild mustangs."

Sarah sprang to her feet and clenched her fists. For the first time since meeting Matthew Sterling, she was thoroughly angry at him. "Don't make fun of me," she cried. "You don't know what it's like to be beholden." Tears of fury fell. "I mean it, Matt. Either you give me worthwhile work to do here on the ranch, or I'm going to Fresno and find a job."

He looked stricken. "I'm sorry, Sarah. I was only teasing you. If you want a job, I have one for you. I've been meaning to mention it, but what with Seth being shot and all, it slipped my mind."

Sarah cocked her head to one side. "What is it? Some made-up something that isn't important?"

Matt gave her a smile. "Not at all. Some of our Mexican workers have children. They help with crops and in the orchards, but are at a great disadvantage because of the language barrier. Do you think you could teach them to speak English? Winter is the perfect time."

Sarah's knees gave way, and she dropped to a nearby settee. "Why, I—"

"Solita will help you," Matt assured her.

"You can do it, Sarah," Seth interrupted. He let out a cowboy yell. "Miss Sarah Joy Anderson's gonna be a schoolmarm!"

Speechless, all she could do was stare. Yet her mind raced like Pandora. She had asked God for work. Matt had offered work that was truly worthwhile. How could she refuse? She closed her eyes and pictured young brown faces turned toward her, shining dark eyes showing eagerness to learn. *Thank You, Lord.*

"How many children will I have?" Sarah asked. "I will need supplies. Slates and chalk and a blackboard so I can draw pictures."

"Only a few families live here year-round. There's fewer than a dozen children right now, ages five to fourteen, in addition to the toddlers and babies. Evan will order whatever supplies you can't find at the general stores. Seth can take you to town tomorrow." Matt grinned. "If it's not too hard a trip for our invalid."

Seth snorted. "Are you crazy? I can't wait to straddle a cayuse again."

"Hold your horses, fire-eater. No cayuses. Take the carriage. You'll need it to bring back Sarah's stuff." Matt stood, crossed the room, and held out a calloused hand. "That is, if it's a deal."

A dozen children? Could she do it? She had to. The only other alternative was a lonely boardinghouse in Fresno where she would never feel safe. "Yes." Sarah put her hand in his. "I don't know how good a teacher I will be, but I promise to work hard."

"That's good enough for me." Matt squeezed her hand then dropped it, but not before Sarah caught a satisfied gleam in his dark blue eyes. "About your salary. . ."

Sarah felt herself redden. "I just need enough for room and board."

"Not on the Diamond S," Matt quietly told her. "Everyone works. Everyone gets paid. You won't make what a regular teacher makes because it will only be for an hour or so a day." He raised his hand when Sarah started to disagree. "No argument. The children have chores, even in winter."

The new schoolmarm subsided. Solita had long since warned her there was no use arguing with Senor Mateo once he made up his mind.

Oh dear! In the discussion with Matt, Sarah had forgotten Solita. She turned to the housekeeper. Her heart thudded to her toes. Solita sat with bowed head. Did she feel it was an insult to the Mexican children to have a girl only a few years older than some of them become their teacher? Sarah rushed to her. "Solita, what is the matter? Don't you want me to teach the children?"

The housekeeper raised her head and blinked back tears. "*Si!* It will make them so happy." She caught Sarah's hand and kissed it. "*Gracias*, senorita. Dios will bless you for your goodness."

Matt said nothing. But his expression when he bade Sarah "Good night" spoke volumes.

eighteen

Two days later Sarah became a teacher. The outfit had turned a vacant storeroom into a schoolroom. Sarah surveyed it with satisfaction. Everything she needed—including her mother's Bible. She tingled with anticipation. After she taught the children to speak English, perhaps she could teach them their *ABC*s.

At nine o'clock sharp, ten excited children took their places. Sarah smiled from behind her new desk, loving the smell of the freshly sawed lumber. "Most of you already know that I am Miss Anderson, but I don't know all your names yet. Tell me so I can write them on the blackboard."

Solita translated into Spanish.

A chorus followed. "José." "Carmelita." "Rosa." "Jorge." "Mateo."

"Mateo?" Sarah eyed the tallest boy suspiciously.

"Si, senorita," he proudly told her.

"His name honors Senor Mateo," Solita explained.

Sarah disciplined a smile and wrote down the rest of the names. Then she picked up her mother's Bible. "Solita, I want to start each day with a Bible story. You will translate."

The housekeeper nodded. "Si. I will make the English words Spanish."

Sarah thrilled at the interest in the attentive faces as she spoke and Solita translated after each sentence.

"David was only a shepherd boy, but God chose him to be a king when he was still a lad, probably no older than you are now, Mateo."

A delighted murmur rippled through the group.

Sarah continued. "God knew that David would one day become a wise king. God may never choose you to be kings, but He has something special for each of you to do. For now it is learning to speak English. Let's bow our heads and pray.

"Dear God, we want to be like David, so we can be whatever You want us to be. In Jesus' name. Amen." A collective *Amen* followed Solita's translation.

"Now we are going to have some fun," Sarah said. Through a combination of gestures and pictures Sarah had drawn on the blackboard, the children learned their first English words. By the end of the first session, the students could understand a few simple instructions such as "stand up" and "sit down."

She could scarcely believe it when Matt stepped inside the open door and said in Spanish, which Solita repeated in English, "Ten o'clock. School's over for today. Did you like it?"

A chorus of, "Si, si! Gracias, senorita. Gracias, senor" left no doubt. Sarah's first day as a teacher was a smashing success. The children clustered around Matt, proudly reciting the English words they had learned.

"That is good. *Adios,*" he told them. "You have chores to do before dinner." Solita shooed them out, and Matt turned to Sarah. A wide grin split his tanned face. "Well? How do you like being a teacher?" he asked in English.

She sank into the chair behind her desk, still excited but suddenly tired. She hadn't fully realized until now how much she wanted to make good in her new job. "I love it. The students— they are so. . ." She couldn't find the words.

Understanding shone in Matt's eyes. "They are God's precious children." He ducked his head and idly made circles on the floor with the toe of his boot. "I have a confession. I eavesdropped."

"You did?" Sarah sat bolt upright. Her pulse quickened.

"Yeah. Good choice of story." A poignant light crept onto his face. "These children need to know they are special." He cleared his throat. "The Diamond S treats them that way, but I can't say the same for everyone in Madera."

Matt's words haunted Sarah long after he left. Head bowed, she prayed, "Dear Lord, please use me to touch the lives of these children. Help me to show how much You love them, so much You sent Your Son to die on the cross for them." A gentle breeze wafted into the silent room like a heavenly benediction—and Sarah rejoiced.

⁂

If Matthew Sterling hadn't already been fathoms deep in love with Sarah, the sight of her conducting school in his home would have sent him head over heels. After eavesdropping on "Sarah's School," as Brett Owen and the hands dubbed it, Matt breathed a prayer. *Someday, Lord, if it be Your plan, Sarah Joy Anderson will be telling Bible stories and pointing our own children to You.* The thought set his heart pounding. The sparkle in Sarah's luminous blue eyes when he asked if she liked teaching was enough to drive a man loco. The vision remained with Matt long after the triangle outside the cook-shack clanged, calling the hands to dinner.

That afternoon Matt rested his hands on the top rail of the corral and watched Sarah lead Pandora out of the barn for their usual afternoon ride. Chase was already saddled and waiting. Matt started toward Sarah, but his three youngest cowboys—all just a little older than Seth—beat him to it. Matt frowned. What were Curly, Bud, and Slim up to?

The trio doffed their Stetsons, then Curly respectfully asked, "Beggin' your pardon, Miss Sarah, but has the boss slapped his brand on you?"

Sarah stared at him as if unable to comprehend. She opened her mouth, but no words came out. Before Matt could bellow at the boys, Bud added, "The reason Curly's askin' is, if the answer's no, then we'd like to carry you to the big doin's in town this weekend."

"Yeah," Slim chimed in, "there's a rodeo an' a square dance an—"

Matt gritted his teeth, but Sarah said, "Carry me? What do you mean?"

Curly whacked his hat against his leg. "Don't pay Bud no mind. He's from Virginny. They talk funny back there. If he were better eddicated, he'da said, take you. Or *es*-cort you. That's more high-toned."

Matt saw Sarah's lips twitch. In spite of his annoyance, he also wanted to laugh. What would the lovable but unpredictable boys do next? More importantly, what would Sarah do?

"Am I to understand all three of you want to escort me?" she demanded.

Astonishment swept over all three faces. Curly—evidently elected spokesman for the group—said, "Why, shore. We're gonna be the three most important fellers there. I'm the best rider and aim to give the boss a run for his money in the men's race. Bud's sure to win either the calf ropin' or the bull ridin'."

Sarah let out a silvery peal of laughter. "What about Slim?"

"He's the modest kind. Don't like to brag, but he's the best square dancer in the outfit," Curly explained. "So, Miss Sarah, are you free to accept our 'nvitation?"

Matt found his tongue. "She is not. Seth and I'll do any *es*-corting there is to do."

Bud stood his ground. "Aw, Boss, we'd be mighty proud to carry her," he protested. " 'Course, if it's hornin' in on you, just say so."

Matt felt trapped between a rock and a hard place. If he said the cowboys were horning in, it would embarrass Sarah.

Keeping silent would put her in a tough position. Inspiration hit him. "It's like this, boys. If Sarah comes sashaying in with the three of you, it will get her in bad with the other girls, especially those who came all by their lonesome. We don't want that to happen, now do we?" The crestfallen escorts looked at each other and shuffled their feet. "Reckon we never thought of that," Curly admitted. A smile broke through the sudden gloom. "Can we at least dance with her?"

Matt laughed. "That is up to the lady."

Three pairs of hopeful eyes turned toward Sarah. She blushed, mounted Pandora, and rode off, but she called back over her shoulder, "The lady says yes."

"*Yippee-ki-ay!* The Diamond S is gonna ride high, wide, and handsome come Saturday," Curly shouted. "Say, Boss, Miss Sarah stays in that saddle as if she'd been born there. Why'n't you get her to ride in the ladies' race? Since the outfit's bent on winnin' all the rodeo prizes, we might as well get one more."

"Good idea, Curly." Matt swung into the saddle and headed in the direction Sarah had taken.

❧

Later that afternoon, Sarah persuaded her brother into taking a walk with her on the pretense she needed to consult him about something. When they stopped beneath a tall cottonwood, she gleefully related her invitation to the "big doin's."

Seth thought it was hilarious. "Those three are my favorites of the outfit, except for Brett Owen. They're such pardners they should have been triplets!" He laughed but quickly sobered. His keen gaze bored into her. "They weren't disrespectful, were they?"

"Oh no! They were polite, funny, and *very* determined to find out if I was wearing Matt's brand. What does that mean, Seth?"

"Out here, an engagement ring stands for a brand—a mark that a girl or young woman is spoken for. Kind of like a No Trespassing sign." Seth hesitated. "Sarah, I don't want to pry, but is Matt going to someday be my real brother?"

"Would you like that?" Sarah held her breath.

"He's the only man I've ever known who is good enough for you. And," he loyally added, "I'll bet my bedroll you're the only woman good enough for him." His face darkened. "Be careful, though, Sarah. Lydia Hensley did a lot of damage to Matt's pride. He thinks a powerful lot of you, and the last thing he needs is to be let down a second time." Seth patted her hand. "Just take your time and be sure." He cleared his throat and changed the subject. "I figured that Gus and Tice would follow you. Wonder why they haven't?"

Sarah shook her head. The fear that lay hidden within her and was sometimes temporarily forgotten flared up like a brush fire. "I don't know."

"If they do come, it probably won't be until spring," Seth comforted. Mischief sprang to his eyes. "Who knows? By then you may have a husband as well as a brother to protect you. What Matt did to Red Fallon isn't a patch on what he'd do to anyone who *really* tried to hurt you."

Sarah grimaced but she kept her thoughts to herself.

❧

Sarah had never been to a rodeo and had no idea what to expect. As usual she sought out Solita. "I know what horse racing is, and calf roping must mean the cowboys are going to rope calves, but why would anyone want to ride a bull?"

Solita's merry laugh bounced off the ceiling of the large, cool kitchen. "You have much to learn if you are to be a rancher's wife, senorita!" The housekeeper's laughter died, and she rolled her expressive dark eyes. "Vaqueros, they are all alike. They ride anything they can straddle, especially bulls. The meaner the better. It is dangerous, very dangerous."

Sarah's mouth dried. She ignored Solita's comment about being a rancher's wife and asked, "Does Matthew do that?"

Solita shook her head. "He only rides in the horse races, and usually he wins."

Sarah sagged with relief. The thought of Matt being trampled by an enraged bull was more than she could bear. She shuddered. "Curly said Bud would either win the calf roping or the bull riding."

"Si. He has won before." Solita patted Sarah's shoulder. "Do not worry, *querida*. We will pray for Senor Bud's safety."

"Matt and Seth want me to enter the ladies' race. Should I? They say Pandora is fast enough to beat almost any horse that runs, but surely there are western girls who ride better than I do."

Solita shrugged. "Perhaps, but you will have fun." She laughed again. "Our Dori won the ladies race when she was fourteen. You will look beautiful in her riding clothes."

Sarah capitulated when she saw the outfit. The expensive riding skirt and vest, high boots, blue silk blouse, and white Stetson fit as if they had been designed for her. And the way Matt looked when he saw her made Sarah feel beautiful.

The rodeo brought out everyone's brightest clothing. The cowboys donned fancy shirts and highly colored neckerchiefs. They polished their boots until they shone, regardless of the fact they would soon be dusty from the events. The ladies decked themselves out in their best gowns. Some carried parasols.

Sarah was delighted to discover her friend Abby from the Yosemite Hotel was going to ride in the ladies' race. "It is so good to see you," the attractive young woman said. "Everyone is glad to know Seth is much better." She cast a furtive glance both ways then leaned close to whisper, "Keep your ears open and your eyes peeled. I heard Red Fallon plans to be here today. He never misses a rodeo."

Sarah gasped. "Surely he wouldn't come after everything he's done!"

"You don't know Red Fallon," Abby warned. "He's likely to turn up anywhere. Besides, even though folks suspect him of shooting your brother, there's no proof." She sighed. "I just wish Sheriff Meade would get some positive evidence that would send Red to the penitentiary!"

The disturbing news cast a cloud over Sarah's day. She alerted Matt and Seth to what she'd learned, but Red didn't appear until the calf roping. To Sarah's disgust he leaped from the saddle of his black stallion, expertly roped and tied the calf, then jumped up with a smirk and threw his hands into the air. A few minutes later, however, Sarah clapped until her hands stung. Bud's time was a few seconds less than Red's. The swaggering cowboy sullenly had to accept second place.

To Sarah's relief Bud didn't enter the bull-riding event. "Stove up my ankle when I hit the ground durin' the calf ropin'," he growled.

"You beat Red," she reminded.

"Yeah." A triumphant gleam shot across Bud's disconsolate face. "Now either Curly or the boss needs to win the men's race. If you win the ladies' race, it'll be frostin' on the cake."

"I'll try," she promised and mounted Pandora for the race. When the horses took off, Sarah bent low over the gelding's neck and screamed encouragement into his ear. Never had he galloped faster. Wind burned Sarah's face and sent her hat flying, along with the hairpins which secured her braids. Her red gold hair streamed behind her like a flame, and the roar of the excited crowd dinned in her ears. On the homestretch Abby's palomino mare kept pace with Pandora. A few yards from the finish line, they surged ahead just enough to win.

"No hard feelings?" Abby asked when they slowed their horses.

"Oh no!" Sarah attempted to smooth her disheveled hair. "That was exciting. But I challenge you to another race sometime."

Abby laughed and held out a gloved hand. "You're on. You're not bad for a tenderfoot. Let's go get our prizes. It's almost time for the men's race."

nineteen

It was not Red Fallon's day. He and his black made a strong showing but only placed third in the men's race. Top honors went to Matt Sterling on Chase and Curly on his favorite buckskin. They were neck and neck all the way and crossed the finish line at the exact same moment.

Red yanked at his horse's reins and gave the winning pair a menacing look that frightened Sarah. So far the Diamond S outfit had studiously avoided him like the plague, but could it last? What if Red showed up at the square dance? There was no telling what might happen.

To Sarah's great relief, Red didn't come. Curly, Bud, and Slim got their turns dancing with her, but most of the time Matt fended off would-be partners by whirling her away. Yet all through the happy evening, a bad feeling niggled at Sarah. Red Fallon was not out of the picture. As the cowboys would say, "Not by a long shot."

❧

One beautiful evening shortly after the rodeo Matt told Sarah there would be no school the next day. Everyone was needed to prepare for a special fiesta in honor of Seth's miraculous recovery.

"What can I do to help?" she inquired.

"Nothing." Matt grinned, the maddening expression that always left her feeling unsettled and wondering what he was thinking. "Why don't you take tomorrow off and do something you really want to do?" He gave her a mock glare. "That does not mean helping Solita!"

Instead of sticking to her guns and reminding Matt she was there to work, as she often did, Sarah obediently said, "All right," then laughed at his look of surprise. She stared west toward a spectacular sunset. Crimson, scarlet, gold, and purple set the skies on fire. "The Bible says red sky in the evening means a fair tomorrow. If it's all right, I will borrow a horse and buggy and go to Madera. I've been wanting to tell Abby and the other girls at the Yosemite Hotel how good God was to spare Seth. There was no chance for a serious talk when I saw them at the rodeo."

Matt looked regretful. "Sorry I can't take you, and Seth's nursing a bum ankle. But one of the boys will be glad to drive for you." Mischief sparkled in his teasing blue eyes. "All of them are more than willing, especially Curly, Bud, and Slim. Of course, choosing one over the others means we will probably have a range war on our hands."

Sarah just laughed and waved away his suggestion, but her pulse quickened.

"Actually I was teasing," Matt said. "One of the men will escort you to town. Just because your stepfather and that gambler haven't showed up yet is no reason to believe they won't—sooner or later."

The next morning, Sarah dressed in her best, blue-checked gingham dress, donned a wide-brimmed hat, and climbed into the buggy Matt had ready and waiting. Curly, clad in a blinding plaid shirt and neckerchief, beamed at her from the driver's seat. "My pards and I tossed a coin to see who got to drive you. I won," he bragged. Sarah couldn't help laughing at his triumphant expression—and at the obviously disgruntled Slim and Bud, who stood nearby.

"Take good care of her, Curly," Matt called when they started off. "*Vaya con* Dios. Sarah, and hurry home."

Go with God. Hurry home. What a beautiful blessing! "We

should be home early in the afternoon," Sarah promised. "Don't eat up all the tamales and enchiladas at dinner." She waved, and they drove away.

Matthew's blessing perched on Sarah's shoulder on her trip to Madera. An occasional lazy hawk circled in the Indian summer sky. A few long-eared jackrabbits with bulging eyes peered at her from beside the road. After Curly made a few unsuccessful attempts to start a conversation, he gave up. It provided the perfect opportunity for Sarah to think and silently talk with her heavenly Father.

Who would have thought the frightened girl who fled from St. Louis would be teaching school on a cattle ranch in California a few months later?

Sarah smiled to herself. Her original ten students had grown to sixteen. After the first few sessions, Carmelita's mother had shyly asked Senor Mateo if "the good Senorita Sarah, who so kindly teaches the muchachos, will also teach the senoras English?" Sarah was aghast. Teaching children was one thing. Teaching their mothers was a different story. Yet the eagerness in the brown-skinned faces awaiting her answer went straight to Sarah's tender heart. These Mexican women were God's children, too. How could she deny them the joy of learning?

She swallowed a lump in her throat and nodded. "Si." All the electric lights that glowed in St. Louis couldn't match the brightness in the women's faces—but the greater reward was Sarah's. The scripture from Luke 6 rang in her ears each time she saw the women struggling to master English and saw their toil-worn fingers painstakingly copying words on the extra slates Matt provided: "*Give, and it shall be given unto you. . . . For with the same measure that ye mete withal it shall be measured to you again.*"

When she mentioned it to Matt, he quietly said, "We can

never out give God, Sarah." He smiled with such obvious approval and love that Sarah felt warmed through and through.

Now as the buggy neared Madera, she silently prayed, *Lord, I am so glad I was able to sow seeds of Christianity during the time I worked at the Yosemite Hotel. I pray they will begin to bear good fruit in the lives of my new friends.* She reflected on how much she had learned to love the country and how much Matt had come to mean in her life. A small smile crept up from her heart. *Thank You, God, for bringing me to California.* She turned to Curly with a bright remark, and they visited the rest of the way to Madera.

Once there, Sarah could hardly wait to see her friends. They left the buggy in a shady grove at the edge of town and agreed to start home around noon.

≈

The din of the metal bar drumming on the triangle announcing the midday meal sounded shortly after Matt rode in from several hours of checking fences.

"About time," Seth complained. "My stomach feels so empty it thinks my throat's been cut."

"Good sign." Matt slapped his dusty Stetson against his boot tops. "If I don't get cleaned up before dinner, Solita will clean my clock." He strode up the wide steps. "Sarah back yet?"

"Naw." Seth raised one eyebrow. "She probably couldn't get away from the girls at the Yosemite Hotel."

"Probably," Matt agreed. But when two o'clock came, he lounged on the shady porch and stared at the road to Madera, nervous as a Mexican jumping bean. Seth had long since settled down for an afternoon *siesta*, obviously untroubled by his sister's absence.

"Don't be stupid," Matt told himself. "Nothing can happen to Sarah when Curly's with her." It didn't help. And when a lathered horse and wild-eyed rider charged into the yard,

Matt cleared the porch steps in one leap.

"Doc Brown says you gotta come quick!" Freckle-faced Johnny Foster gasped for breath. "Curly's hurt bad. He was found knocked out cold in an alley. Nobody knows how long he'd been there."

Heart thundering, Matt grabbed Johnny's shoulder. "What about Sarah?"

"Seth's sister?" Johnny looked surprised. "I don't know anything about her."

In the time it took to saddle Chase and a fresh horse for Johnny, something inside Matt died.

Every pound of the horses' hooves on the way to Madera echoed the beat of his worried heart. "Lord," he prayed, low enough that Johnny couldn't hear, "You know my life will be meaningless without Sarah. Please be with her, wherever she is."

It seemed like a century before they reached Madera and Doc Brown. Curly had just regained consciousness, face pale beneath a heavy bandage around his head.

"Where's Sarah?" Matt challenged.

"Sarah?" Curly groggily shook his head and winced. "Probably still at the hotel. I remember starting to meet her before noon. I passed an alley and woke up here in Doc's office...."

Matt was already rushing for the door, heart in his throat. *God, is Sarah at the hotel? If so, surely she would have heard about Curly and gotten word to me!* Fortunately Abby was on duty.

"Sarah? She went to meet Curly just before noon," Abby said. "Maybe they stopped off to see someone."

Fear spurted. "Who does Sarah know?" Matt demanded.

Abby laughed. "Everyone knows and loves Sarah. She could be at the post office or the minister's or—"

"Thanks," Matt cut in. He forced a smile over the rising

suspicion that something was terribly wrong. Not everyone loved Sarah. He could name three without thinking: Gus Stoddard, Tice Edwards, Red Fallon. Well, Stoddard and Edwards were far away, but Red might still be around.

Matt felt sick. He turned on his heel and headed for the sheriff's office. "Whoever knocked Curly out did it for a reason," he told Sheriff Meade. "I'm dead sure that reason is Sarah."

A thorough search of the small town turned up no sign of the young woman or the buggy. The sheriff hastily organized a posse. The questioning of citizens began in earnest. No one had seen or heard a thing about Sarah.

Helplessness fell on Matt like a saddle blanket on Chase's back. There were no clues to Sarah's disappearance. Matt only knew she hadn't taken the road back to the ranch. He would have passed her on his way to Madera. Sick at heart, he bowed his head. His anguish-filled mind repeated over and over, *Where is Sarah?*

❧

Sarah had a wonderful time visiting with her friends at the Yosemite Hotel, including Captain Russell Perry Mace. The captain's hints about what an exemplary man Matthew Sterling was and the assurance her job would be open in the spring "if she needed it" failed to get a commitment from Sarah. His words did, however, make her anxious to get back to the ranch. Her reflections during her ride into town had helped Sarah realize her feelings for Matt were genuine and did not spring from a desire to escape from Tice. Her prayers had led her to believe that Matt was the man with whom God wanted her to spend the rest of her life. Matthew had patiently given her the time she requested to be sure, but now she couldn't wait to tell him she had never been more certain of anything in her life. Her heart felt lighter than a spring morning. Was any woman ever so blessed as she?

When Curly didn't come for her at the appointed time, Sarah figured he must have misunderstood their meeting place and would be waiting for her at the buggy. She strolled to the grove of shade trees at the edge of town. The buggy sat waiting. The carriage horse, tethered so he could graze, nickered a welcome, but there was no sign of Curly.

Sarah laughed and hitched the horse to the buggy. "Curly probably ran into a friend and lost track of time," she mused. "He will be along soon." She sat down in the shade and closed her eyes, lost in anticipation of seeing Matt soon.

Her joy was short-lived. All too soon, a coarse voice interrupted her reverie.

"Well, lookee who's here."

Sarah's eyes jerked open. Red Fallon grinned down at her from atop his black horse. There was no mistaking his coarse red hair, beard, and leering face.

Sarah's ballooning spirits fell to the ground as if punctured.

"I want a word with you."

A spurt of fear shot through Sarah. She looked around for help, but no one was in sight. "I have nothing to say to you." She stood then sprang into the buggy. Lightly flicking the horse with the reins, she urged him forward.

Her attempt to escape was futile. Red vaulted to the ground and onto the buggy seat in two gigantic leaps. Then he pulled a pistol. "None of that, missy. I'd as soon knock you out as look at you." He snatched up the reins with his free hand, leaving his mount to follow behind. "I reckon I'll ride a piece with you."

Red whipped the horse, and they sped away from town—at far too fast a pace for Sarah to risk jumping from the rig.

When Sarah could find her voice, she summoned her iciest manner. "I demand an explanation. Why are you doing this?"

Red smiled wickedly. "Just doing my job," he mumbled.

Doing his job? A horrid feeling engulfed Sarah. It couldn't be! Surely Gus and Tice were not involved in her abduction. Here? After all these months? It seemed impossible that they would have followed her all the way to Madera and then been able to keep their presence a secret.

Determined to learn the worst, Sarah pushed for the truth. "And just what is this job?" she demanded.

"I met some men from St. Louis, old friends of your'n, in Fresno," he bragged. "Yore daddy and your heartbroken fiancé—Edwards, isn't it? What'd you mean runnin' off like that?" He didn't wait for a reply but rambled on, obviously getting perverse pleasure from the situation. Every word from his cruel mouth brought despair.

"No one makes a fool outa Red Fallon," he sneered. "I alwuz git even." He whipped the horse into a dead run, and his eyes gleamed.

A few miles south of Madera, Red halted the buggy. Standing in the middle of the road was a horse-drawn coach and two men: Gus Stoddard and Tice Edwards smiling in a way that curdled Sarah's blood.

Tice yanked her out of the buggy. "I've lost a lot of time and money tracking you down," he shouted, "more than you're worth."

Sarah felt sick. Her heart fluttered in fear. "How did you find me?" she whispered.

He sneered. "Gus found a barely legible letter from Seth under your bed."

Sarah gasped. Seth's missing letter!

Tice cursed. "Unfortunately there were no clues to his whereabouts. Worse, the postmark was so blurred that all we could make out was *M-a-something, California*."

Tice shook his fist in Sarah's face. "Have you any idea how

much it costs to send telegrams to 'Seth Anderson,' in care of every post office in California that starts with the letters *M* and *a*?"

He blew out a breath as putrid as himself. "None of them did any good. We've spent weeks crisscrossing this rotten state. If we hadn't run across Fallon when we stopped at a saloon in Fresno on our way here, we'd still be looking for you. When we're back in St. Louis, you'll pay, Sarah Anderson!"

She shuddered. Any true feelings the man might have had for her had clearly worn away over the past months. Only Tice's pride and Gus's outstanding gambling debt had kept them searching for the ungrateful girl. Clenching her fingers until the nails bit into the palms of her hands, Sarah defied them. "I am not going back to St. Louis. And I will never be your wife."

"Oh, I think you will," Tice said silkily. He reached into his waistcoat, brought out a goodly amount of money, and thrust it at Red. "Here you are. If anyone asks what's become of Sarah, tell them her father and her husband came to get her."

Red's jaw dropped. "Husband! And her carryin' on with Matt Sterling? Well, whadda you know!"

"Oh yes." Tice took out a paper and flourished it before Red's amazed eyes. "See? A marriage certificate, all signed and proper. Wonder what your Matt Sterling's going to say when he hears he's been courting a married woman?"

twenty

Tice Edwards waved the sham marriage certificate under Sarah's nose. Triumph and hatred made his eyes more snakelike than ever. "Did you hear that, *Mrs. Edwards*? You think you're such a high and mighty Christian, better than honest men like your daddy and me. Bah!" He spat in the dusty road. "According to Fallon here, you've been acting all sweet and *available*, all the while being my wife." He donned a pious expression that made Sarah's stomach lurch. "Good thing Gus and I found you when we did. Sounds like we got here just before you up and married this Sterling in spite of already having a husband."

Gus Stoddard let out a coarse "haw-haw." The delight in Red Fallon's gloating face was enough to send arrows of fear winging into Sarah's heart. Never in her life had she encountered such evil. Yet part of her wanted to shriek with laughter at Tice's hypocrisy, although the knowledge that his slick tongue could charm a den of rattlesnakes added terror to her situation. What should she do? She was no match for even one of these wicked men, let alone the three together in cahoots against her.

A heavily marked verse in Virginia Anderson's Bible flashed into Sarah's mind: *"Submit yourselves therefore to God. Resist the devil, and he will flee from you."* It was so strong it swept away some of Sarah's fear. Isaiah 54:17 quickly followed, the beloved verse Sarah had relied on in her wild flight from St. Louis to Madera: *"No weapon that is formed against thee shall prosper. . . . This is the heritage of the servants of the Lord."*

A silent prayer shot skyward. *God, I have submitted myself to You. I am Your servant. I claim Your promise, which is my heritage. I don't know how You are going to free me, but I trust that You will. Perhaps even now Matthew and the outfit are looking for me. In the meantime. . .*

Tice roughly grabbed Sarah's shoulder. "Well?" The word cracked like a rifle shot. "What have you to say for yourself?"

Red Fallon cackled. "More like a mountain lion when you get her riled." He rubbed the cheek that had worn the prints of Sarah's fingers.

Tice's eyes gleamed with anticipation. "All the better. More fun to tame her that way."

The men's suggestive laughter sent fury cascading through Sarah. She tore herself away from Tice's painful grip, opened her mouth to shrivel them with words then stopped. A plan had popped into her head with the speed of a bullet. There was a far better way. She turned her back on Tice and Red. If the idea were to work, it must be through Gus. He loved money more than anything in the world. Could she play on his greed?

"I know I've caused you a lot of trouble," she told him.

Gus's mouth gaped, disclosing his stained teeth, but she rushed on.

"I can make it up to you, Gus."

Her stepfather's disbelieving snort boded no good for Sarah's plan. "You can make it up to me by marryin' Tice. You shoulda done it in the first place 'nsteada runnin' off out here."

Sarah drew herself to her full height. "Matthew Sterling is the owner of the Diamond S Ranch, the biggest spread in the valley. He's rich and the most respected man in this part of the state. If you release me, he will pay you far more than Tice will ever give you. I promise you that."

Tice bellowed with rage, but Sarah saw the telltale avarice spring to Gus's eyes. "What makes you think this rancher would do that for the likes o' you?" he said suspiciously.

"Matt will do whatever it takes to get me back." Knowledge it was true rang in every word. If it took everything Matt Sterling possessed, he would gladly give it away to free her.

Gus turned to Tice. "If he's that rich, it might not be a bad idee," he tentatively said. "You can get any woman you want, and we wouldn't have a kidnapping charge hangin' over our heads."

"Kidnapping!" Red Fallon cursed. "You didn't say anythin' about this bein' a kidnapping. Is she your wife or ain't she?"

"Sure she is," Tice lied. "Can't you tell she's just trying to work us against each other? She's having pipe dreams about Sterling. Besides, if he's all that respectable and looked up to, he's not going to pay out good money when he finds it's for another man's wife."

A surge of courage caused Sarah to say, "Don't believe him, Red. It's a wicked lie. I am not his wife, and Gus Stoddard isn't my father. He sold me to Tice to pay his gambling debts."

Her hopes of enlisting Red's aid died aborning. He raised one eyebrow and said, "I reckon I'll believe the feller what paid me for helpin' him." He held out a soiled paw and solemnly shook Tice's smooth hand then smirked at Sarah. He quickly mounted the black horse that had followed behind Matt's horse and buggy. "So long, Sarah Anderson Edwards. I'll make sure to announce yore marriage," he mockingly called as he rode back the way he had brought Sarah.

Sarah was aghast. With him went all hope for escape. Even if Gus believed Matt would pay a ransom for her, he was too weak to stand up against Tice. Once they got to Fresno, Gus and Tice would hustle her aboard the train. All would be lost. If she tried to enlist help, they would produce the forged marriage certificate and make up some plausible story about her not being well and unable to know what she was saying.

"We better get outa here," Gus muttered, peering fearfully into the rapidly falling shadows. "If Sarah ain't lyin' about Sterling, we may have a posse on our trail."

Tice shoved Sarah inside the coach, waited for Gus to climb aboard, then jumped to the driver's seat and urged the horses faster and faster through the darkening evening. The two lighted lanterns barely gave enough light to penetrate the growing gloom that hovered between sunset and the appearance of moon or stars, but Tice didn't slow the horses. He whipped them unmercifully and swore when they could run no faster.

Sarah clung to the side of the rocking coach to keep from being tossed about. Where would it all end? They rounded a sharp turn. Sarah screamed.

A deer stood in the middle of the road, transfixed by the lantern light.

The horses whinnied and reared. "Get out of the way, you—" A string of curses followed. Tice lost control of the carriage. It slammed into a boulder at the side of the road and overturned.

Sarah's last conscious thought as she was hurled from the coach was a silent cry: *This is the end, God. At least You saved me from Tice. I'm just sorry I never got to tell Matt how much I care for him.*

❧

Earlier that day Matt and Sheriff Meade and his posse had conducted a thorough search for Sarah. It was no use. She had vanished as if spirited away by the wind. Tired and discouraged they turned back to town.

While they were riding down the street, Evan Moore rushed into the street and waved them down.

"Red Fallon's in the saloon. He's spinning a yarn about getting even with you and the tenderfoot you took in." Dread etched deep lines in the postmaster's face. "I'm afraid it might have something to do with Miss Sarah being missing."

Matt leaped from Chase. "It had better not. If Red's up to his old tricks, I'll break every bone in his body!" His long strides took him down the street ahead of the others and into the saloon with a crash of the swinging doors. "Fallon?"

"Right here." Red gave a drunken laugh and jingled a handful of money, more money than he should have on him this far from payday.

Matt collared him and bellowed, "Do you know anything about Sarah Anderson?"

Red crowed with glee. "A lot more than you do, Matthew Sterling. All this time you been sparkin' her, she's been married!" He gave a fiendish laugh and pointed an accusing finger. "I reckon that'll tie a knot in your lasso. She ain't Miss Sarah Anderson a'tall. She's *Mrs. Tice Edwards!*"

"That's a rotten lie," Matt shouted. "Who told you such a monstrous thing?"

Red burst into laughter again. "Her daddy and her husband. That's who!"

A collective gasp went up from the hangers-on in the saloon. Matt, although shocked to the core to learn Tice Edwards had found Sarah, kept a tight rein on himself. If he could string Red along, perhaps the despicable cowhand would spill his guts with more details—especially the whereabouts of Sarah and her companions. "How'd you happen to make the acquaintance of Tice Edwards?"

Drunk as much with success at finally besting Matt as by being "likkered up," Red was triumphant. "Met him an' Gus Stoddard in Fresno. Gossip had it they were tryin' to find Sarah. I told 'em for a consideration I'd help them. They were all torn up over her havin' run away from home."

Matt could barely breathe. "You helped kidnap Sarah?"

Red's face flamed, and he shook himself free from Matt's clutch. "Naw! There was no kidnapping to it! I just took Sarah to her daddy and her husband. There's a real happy endin'. Right now they're in a coach bigger than yours, on their way back to St. Louis." Red guffawed. " 'Course that cuts you out, Matt. Lady Luck ain't very good to you when it comes to love, is she? This is the second time a little ol' gal has made a fool of you!"

After getting a fuller description of the coach from Red, Matt had heard all he needed to know. *Crack*. A well-placed punch left Red sprawled on the saloon floor. Matt towered over him. "Listen, Red, and listen hard. Either you leave the valley for good, or I'm swearing out a warrant for kidnapping." He ignored Red's protest. "Sarah Anderson is not and never has been married to Tice Edwards. If she'll have me, I aim to make her my wife. Even if she were married, your waylaying her could send you to jail for a long time. Right, sheriff?" He turned to Sheriff Meade, who had arrived in time to see Red hit the floor.

"That's right," the sheriff seconded. "You've plumb wore out what little welcome you ever had in Madera. Now git up, and git before I run you in!"

Red slunk out but not before giving them both a baleful look.

⚞

Now that Matt knew Gus and Tice's destination, he rode toward Fresno as if pursued by a thousand howling devils. Chase fully lived up to his name. The buckskin gelding had never run faster or more smoothly. They reached the buggy in which Sarah and Curly had driven to Madera. The horse was still in the traces. Matt freed him but didn't attempt to lead him. He would only slow Chase down. Instead Matt staked him out by a patch of nearby grass. He'd retrieve the horse and buggy after he found Sarah.

Daylight gave way to growing darkness, but there was still no sign of the girl Matt loved. He slowed Chase and gave thanks for the multitude of brilliant stars that lighted their way. Then, around a bend in the road, Matt came across a gruesome scene: an overturned coach, with the horses still in their harness. The driver sprawled across the seat. Dead. The coach fit the description he'd gotten from Red.

Matt yanked the coach door open. A battered and bleeding older man—Gus Stoddard, no doubt—fell into his arms. The coach was empty. Matt's world turned black. "Where's Sarah?" he demanded, torn between rage and a reluctant pity for the injured man.

"I don't know." Gus was incoherent. Blood flowed freely, but a quick examination showed his injuries didn't appear to be life threatening. Gus Stoddard would live to return to his family.

Matt gave a cry of despair. "Sarah, where are you?"

The silence was so profound Matt could hear his breaking heart thunder in his chest.

twenty-one

Matthew Sterling fell to his knees beside the coach and faced his own personal Gethsemane. How could God take Sarah and let worthless Gus Stoddard live? From the looks of the overturned coach, it had been traveling at a terrible pace. He would find Sarah somewhere in the darkness, lifeless and broken. Despair descended like a woolen blanket, smothering Matt until he wondered if he would survive. He beat his fists on the ground. Guilt tormented him. He had promised Seth to protect his beloved sister—and failed. "I should have taken Sarah to Madera and let the ranch chores go hang," he cried out.

Memories rose to haunt him: Sarah as a young girl in the picture in Seth's saddlebags. Sarah miraculously transformed into the woman whose picture Matt carried just over his heart. Sarah at the Yosemite Hotel, eyes filled with gratitude for what Matt had done for her brother. Sarah on Pandora. Sarah with Seth. With Solita. With Curly, Bud, and Slim, who were outspoken in their admiration. The courageous girl repelling Red Fallon's advances. Finally Sarah teaching the Mexican children and their mothers, face alight with the joy of giving.

Matt had thought he loved her beyond description, praying she would be God's choice to complete his life. Yet those feelings were nothing compared with what he now felt— when it was too late. She had asked for time to be sure of her own feelings. He had given it to her. She must not marry him out of gratitude or the need for a protector. She must explore her heart before she wore the gold band of wifehood.

Now there was no time for Sarah to learn to love him the

way he believed she had begun to do. No time to place the sparkling engagement ring that had belonged to Matt's mother on Sarah's finger—the ring he had never considered offering to Lydia Hensley. Matt groaned, the sound loud in the quiet spot. "Why, God?" The night remained still, as if holding its breath, waiting for an answer or silently mourning a life snatched away by lust and greed. A rustle of leaves came, and a low cry as soft as an angel's wing.

"Matthew? Thank God. I knew you'd come!"

Matt leaped up, snatched a lantern, and strode toward the sound of Sarah's voice. She lay in a crumpled heap in the shadows at the side of the road, dirty and disheveled. One sleeve of her blue and white gingham dress was torn. A dark bruise and a trickle of dried blood on her forehead showed in the flickering light.

Matt set the lantern down and peered at her. How badly was she hurt? *Please, God, don't let her have broken her back when she was thrown from the coach.* "Can you move your legs and arms?" he asked.

"I think so." She struggled to a sitting position and smiled weakly.

Relief gushed through Matt like water through a sieve. He caught Sarah in his arms and held her against his out-of-control heart. "I thought I'd lost you!"

A dirty but sturdy hand stroked his tear-stained face. "You won't have to, Matthew. When Tice lost control of the coach, I knew I was going to die. My last thought was regret that I didn't have the chance to tell you I've come to love you with all my heart."

Too overcome with emotion to speak, Matt tenderly kissed her and thanked God.

❧

Any lingering doubts Sarah may have had about her love for

Matt vanished forever with their first real kiss. She returned it with all her heart then nestled in his arms, feeling like she had come home after a long, arduous journey. "How did you find me?"

"I had a little talk with your old friend, Red Fallon."

Sarah gasped. "What did you do to him?"

"Gave him a quick punch to remember me by then told him to pack up and leave Madera or get jailed for kidnapping."

A moan brought Sarah back to the present. Filled with dread, she quavered, "Gus? Tice?"

Matt placed his hands on each side of her troubled face. "Gus isn't seriously hurt, but Tice is dead."

Sarah slumped against him, feeling she had received a stay of execution. Never again would the riverboat gambler have power over her, even false power granted by those in high places who were as unscrupulous as himself. "Was he killed instantly?"

Matt sounded reluctant to tell her when he said, "It appears Tice's neck was broken when the coach turned over."

Sarah shuddered and grasped Matt's strong hands. "The last thing I heard before Tice lost control of the carriage and it slammed into the boulder at the side of the road was him cursing the horses. Would he have had time to ask for God's mercy before he died?"

"We'll never know," Matt quietly told her. "I hated Tice, but God help the man if Tice carried his sins into eternity." Matt cleared his throat. "We need to head home. The coach is no use to us. We'll ride Chase double. Gus will have to ride one of the coach horses. When we reach the place where Red Fallon left the horse and buggy, we'll be right as rain."

Sarah jerked her attention from Tice Edwards's fate to the present. She hadn't told Matt that every bone in her body hurt. Could she ride, even surrounded by Matt's protective arms? She had to. *"I can do all things through Christ which strengtheneth me,"* she silently quoted, trying not to limp when Matt helped her to her feet. She needn't have worried about him noticing. He stepped toward Gus, who lay moaning and cursing where Matt had left him earlier.

"Don't stand there like a blitherin' idjit, girl. Git over here and help me!" Gus barked. Another string of curses followed.

"Shut your dirty mouth, or I'll gag you and leave you here," Matt threatened. "The only reason you'll get any help is so I can turn you over to the sheriff. And you'll get no help from Sarah, ever again." He hoisted Gus to a standing position.

"I didn't do nothin' wrong," Gus whined. "Who're you, anyway, to interfere with a man and his daughter? I come all the way from St. Louis to fetch Sarah home. By all that's holy, that's what I'm gonna do." He put on an innocent air that sickened Sarah. "Tice is dead which means I ain't owin' him anything. Sarah, you've got no reason for not comin' home. Your daddy and the young-uns need lookin' after."

The relief Sarah had felt when she heard the miserable wretch was still alive changed to outrage. "Gus Stoddard, you aren't my father, and you know it! Never in this world would my mother have put you in charge of me." Contempt for the pitiful excuse of a man underscored every word. "Your trumped-up claims are more worthless than Confederate money." She paused, caught her breath, and drew herself to her full height. "This is my betrothed, Matthew Sterling. He has Sheriff Meade and half the men in Madera out looking for me."

Gus sneered. "What'd that good-for-nothin' Fallon do? Spill his guts?"

"Oh yeah," Matt told him. "Mighty proud he was of helping Sarah's 'brokenhearted daddy and fiancé' find her. You must have been mighty convincing, but you don't sway me. You'll have a snowball's chance in August of making Sheriff Meade swallow your yarn. This is the last time you'll stalk Sarah, Stoddard. Try it again, and I'll see that you get everything that's coming to you. If Edwards had lived, he'd have found out how the code of the West deals with citified dandies who bother our women."

Gus cringed, as if each word were a heavy blow to his hapless head. How quickly he lost his false bravado when confronted by a real man, Sarah thought.

Matt freed the horses still harnessed to the overturned coach and quickly fashioned crude hackamores from the reins. "Time to be on our way."

"I can't ride no horse bareback," Gus grumbled.

"Quit bellyaching and suit yourself. You can either ride bareback, or I'll tie you." Matt reached for the lariat coiled on Chase's saddle.

Gus glared at him, face sullen in the dim light. "No one's ropin' me to a horse." Groaning and complaining, he managed to get astride one of the coach horses and cling to the rude hackamore. He mercifully fell silent when they got to the Diamond S horse and buggy and clambered in for the ride back to Madera, which was closer than the ranch. Matt drove, leaving Chase and the other horses to tag along behind. But the moment the first lights of town became visible, Gus vaulted from the buggy and disappeared into the night.

"Shall I go after him?" Matt asked Sarah.

She sighed. The thought of Gus being in California left her shaken, but— "Let him go. He will find someone to fleece or lend him money enough to go back to Missouri. He'll spruce himself up and court some well-to-do woman who won't see through him."

Matt helped her down from the buggy. "You look all

tuckered out. First we see Doc Brown then the captain. You can stay at the hotel until you feel like coming out to the ranch." A poignant light darkened his blue eyes. "Just don't make it too long."

Sarah's heart gave a little skip. "I won't. Right now all I want is food and a bed." She looked down at her filthy hands and dress. "Mercy, the captain won't want me dirtying up his nice hotel. I must look a sight."

Matt cupped her face in his hands. "If we live to be a hundred, you will never be more beautiful to me than you are right now," he said huskily.

"Dirt and all?"

"Dirt and all." A teasing look crept into his face. "A little dirt never hurt a rancher's wife."

Long after Matthew headed back to the ranch, Sarah treasured his words and hugged to herself the joy in store for her as mistress of the Diamond S.

&

It took Sarah two days to get over her stiffness and soreness enough to leave the Yosemite Hotel. She chafed at the delay but was amazed to discover God had a reason for her to be there: her friend Abby. Along with clean clothing, Abby provided information that sent Sarah's spirits sky-high.

"When we discovered you were missing, I got the girls together," Abby said. Tears sparkled in her dark eyes. "Some of us don't know God very well, but we figured He'd listen since we were praying for you."

Sarah took Abby's hands in hers. "Your prayers were answered. If it hadn't been for God, I wouldn't be alive. Anytime you want to know Him better, all you have to do is tell Him so." Desire for her friend to experience the love and caring of their heavenly Father spilled out. "Abby, He is the only One who can save you, and you will never have a better friend. When Jesus is in your heart, it doesn't matter if others persecute you. Once you are His, nothing can harm you unless He allows it."

Longing filled Abby's sweet face. "It sounds wonderful." She sniffled. "When I found out you were missing, I thought I'd go crazy, but it's like you're at peace no matter what. Sarah, what must I do to get what you have?"

"Paul tells the Romans in chapter 10: 'If thou shalt confess with thy mouth the Lord Jesus, and shalt believe in thine heart that God hath raised him from the dead, thou shalt be saved.'"

"It sounds awfully simple."

Sarah's heart throbbed with gladness. "The way of salvation is a free gift and so simple even a child can understand. Do you want to accept Him?"

Abby nodded. A few heartbeats later a new name was written in the Book of Life.

When Sarah got back to the ranch and told Matt and Seth the good news, she added, "I didn't dream God would bring good from Tice and Gus coming out here after me. Or from Red Fallon waylaying me." She blinked back tears of joy. "If they hadn't, Abby wouldn't have accepted the Lord, at least not right now."

"Another good thing came out of it," Matt told her when they mounted Chase and Pandora and rode out together later that day. At the foot of the promontory they both loved, Matt halted Chase and took Sarah's hand. "Sarah, when will you marry me?"

She cocked her head to one side and pretended to consider. "I believe the proper length for an engagement is a year—"

"Are you really going to make me wait that long when it feels like I've been waiting for you my whole life?" Mischief danced in his eyes. "If you'd come sooner, I wouldn't have been tricked into thinking Lydia Hensley was pure gold, not just iron pyrite—*fool's gold.*"

Sarah threw caution to the winds. "Senor Mateo, if you'll give Pandora and me a head start to the big oak tree and still beat us back to the ranch, I'll marry you whenever you choose!" She touched her heels to the chestnut gelding's smooth sides, and laughter floated back over her shoulder.

Matt erupted into a shout of glee worthy of an Indian on the warpath. He waited until the fleeing pair reached the oak tree then sent Chase into a full gallop. Despite Pandora's best efforts, Chase caught and passed him just before they reached the corral. Matt reined in, leaped from the saddle, caught Sarah as she slid down from the gelding, and announced to the crowd of staring, openmouthed cowboys nearby, "Don't make any plans for Christmas. We're gonna have a wedding, and you no-good, lazy cowpunchers are all invited!"

Matt threw his hat in the air and let out another war whoop, echoed by the grinning outfit. He whipped around toward Curly and pounded his shoulder. "Saddle up. I need you to ride into Madera and send a telegram to Dori. This is one Christmas on the Diamond S my sister had better not miss!"

๛

Once upon a time, Sarah Joy Anderson had stood for the final fitting of a wedding gown she hated. Her fingers had itched to tear it off and throw it in the dressmaker's smug face. Instead she had closed her eyes and wondered what it would be like to walk up the aisle of the church in Madera and find Matthew Sterling waiting for her.

Months later Matt had unwittingly described Sarah's dream: *"Someday you're going to walk up the aisle of our Madera church on Seth's arm, all gussied up in a fluffy white dress and ready to become Mrs. Matthew Sterling."*

On Christmas Day the dream became reality. Sarah wore no fancy, pearl-beaded gown but Matt's grandmother's carefully preserved wedding dress. No veil with orange blossoms decked Sarah's hair but a gorgeous lace mantilla Solita provided. No gawkers marred the occasion. Instead a host of smiling well-wishers crowded the church. They included a lovely, dark-haired girl in an elegant blue velvet cloak. She had arrived on the westbound train and been enveloped in a joyous bear hug from her bridegroom brother.

ぉ

"Ready?" Seth grinned. "You don't want to keep Matt waiting."

Sarah nudged him. "Just remember, your turn's coming." She sent a pointed glance toward Dori Sterling, seated in the front row with Solita.

Seth retaliated by whispering, "Naw. She's too Bostonish, and I'm just a poor, lonesome cowpoke." He smirked. "Get a move on, will you, before Matt changes his mind."

Sarah placed a lace-mitted hand on Seth's arm. The wonder and love in Matthew Sterling's face showed Seth's warning was foolishness. The Sierra Nevada would crumble to dust before the boss of the Diamond S would go back on Sarah Joy Anderson.

Thank You, God, for bringing us here, even though it was by long and tortuous paths. Thank You most of all for the gift of Your Son, whose birthday we celebrate this day. No matter how rough the trails ahead of us may be, we can ride them together because Jesus goes before us.

Fortified by the prayer, secure in God's and Matt's love, Sarah squeezed Seth's arm and started up the aisle. Each step brought her closer to the man in the faded photograph now pinned beneath her wedding dress—Matthew Sterling, who had lassoed her heart.

A Note from the Author:

God uses many ways to lead His children, including through the written word. I learned to read by kerosene lamplight. One night I said, "I wish we had a magic lamp and a magic carpet like Aladdin." My parents pointed out that our new lamp was an "Aladdin" lamp and that books were our magic carpet. I vowed to someday write a book of my own.

In 1977 I wanted to write for God. He used a passage from Emilie Loring's *There is Always Love* to encourage me: "There is only one common-sense [sic] move when you don't like your life. Do something about it. Get out. Go somewhere. Follow a rainbow. Who knows? You may find the legendary pot of gold at the end of it." I walked off my government job a few days later.

My "someday" book has grown to more than 140 titles and six million copies sold. Many, such as *Frontiers* and *Frontier Brides* (Barbour books) were inspired by Dad's love of western lore. How my eleven-year-old heart pounded when I saw my first cowboy. If only I could live on a cattle ranch! (I still hope to visit one.)

I hope you get as much pleasure from reading this story as I did writing it.

Blessings,
Colleen

A Letter To Our Readers

Dear Reader:
In order that we might better contribute to your reading enjoyment, we would appreciate your taking a few minutes to respond to the following questions. We welcome your comments and read each form and letter we receive. When completed, please return to the following:

Fiction Editor
Heartsong Presents
PO Box 719
Uhrichsville, Ohio 44683

1. Did you enjoy reading *Romance Rides the Range* by Colleen L. Reece?
   ❏ Very much! I would like to see more books by this author!
   ❏ Moderately. I would have enjoyed it more if

   _____

   _____

   _____

2. Are you a member of **Heartsong Presents**? ❏ Yes ❏ No
   If no, where did you purchase this book? _____

   _____

3. How would you rate, on a scale from 1 (poor) to 5 (superior), the cover design? _____

4. On a scale from 1 (poor) to 10 (superior), please rate the following elements.

   ____ Heroine   ____ Plot
   ____ Hero   ____ Inspirational theme
   ____ Setting   ____ Secondary characters

5. These characters were special because? _____
   _____
   _____

6. How has this book inspired your life? _____
   _____
   _____

7. What settings would you like to see covered in future
   Heartsong Presents books? _____
   _____
   _____

8. What are some inspirational themes you would like to see
   treated in future books? _____
   _____
   _____

9. Would you be interested in reading other **Heartsong
   Presents** titles? ❑ Yes   ❑ No

10. Please check your age range:
    ❑ Under 18   ❑ 18-24
    ❑ 25-34   ❑ 35-45
    ❑ 46-55   ❑ Over 55

Name _____
Occupation _____
Address _____
City, State, Zip _____
E-mail _____

FREEDOM'S CROSSROAD

3 stories in 1

The young women feel they have been abandoned by God. Forgiveness is the key to freedom for three brokenhearted women.

Historical, paperback, 368 pages, 5 3/16" x 8"

Hearts♥ong

Presents

Great Inspirational Romance at a Great Price!

Heartsong Presents books are inspirational romances in contemporary and historical settings, designed to give you an enjoyable, spirit-lifting reading experience. You can choose wonderfully written titles from some of today's best authors like Wanda E. Brunstetter, Mary Connealy, Susan Page Davis, Cathy Marie Hake, Joyce Livingston, and many others.

When ordering quantities less than twelve, above titles are $2.97 each.
Not all titles may be available at time of order.

SEND TO: **Heartsong Presents** Readers' Service
P.O. Box 721, Uhrichsville, Ohio 44683
Please send me the items checked above. I am enclosing $ _____
(please add $4.00 to cover postage per order. OH add 7% tax. WA
add 8.5%). Send check or money order, no cash or C.O.D.s, please.
To place a credit card order, call 1-740-922-7280.

NAME _____

ADDRESS _____

CITY/STATE _____ ZIP_____

HEARTSONG
PRESENTS

If you love Christian romance...

$10.^{99}$

You'll love Heartsong Presents' inspiring and faith-filled romances by today's very best Christian authors...Wanda E. Brunstetter, Mary Connealy, Susan Page Davis, Cathy Marie Hake, and Joyce Livingston, to mention a few!

When you join Heartsong Presents, you'll enjoy four brand-new, mass-market, 176-page books—two contemporary and two historical—that will build you up in your faith when you discover God's role in every relationship you read about!

Imagine...four new romances every four weeks—with men and women like you who long to meet the one God has chosen as the love of their lives...all for the low price of $10.99 postpaid.

To join, simply visit www.heartsong presents.com or complete the coupon below and mail it to the address provided.

Mass Market 176 Pages